MONSTER ODYSSEY

THE EYE OF NEPTUNE

JON MAYHEW

BLOOMSBURY

LONDON NEW DELHI NEW YORK SYDNEY

For Mum and Dad,
who would have loved such nonsense!

Bloomsbury Publishing, London, New Delhi, New York and Sydney

First published in Great Britain in May 2013 by Bloomsbury Publishing Plc
50 Bedford Square, London WC1B 3DP

Text copyright © Jon Mayhew 2013

The moral right of the author has been asserted

A CIP catalogue record for this book is available from the British Library

ISBN 978 1 4088 2630 0

1 3 5 7 9 10 8 6 4 2

MIX
Paper from
responsible sources
FSC® C020471

Typeset by Hewer Text UK Ltd, Edinburgh
Printed and bound in Great Britain by CPI Group (UK) Ltd, Croydon CR0 4YY

www.bloomsbury.com
www.JonMayhewBooks.com

'Let me tell you . . . you won't regret the time you spend aboard my vessel. You're going to voyage through a land of wonders. Stunned amazement will probably be your habitual state of mind.'

Jules Verne, *Twenty Thousand Leagues Under the Sea*

PROLOGUE
LIVERPOOL, 1810

I hate this place, Prince Dakkar thought, pressing himself against a dirty, soot-stained brick wall. *It's cold and grey. The English are cold and grey!*

He shivered, watching people squeeze past each other, wrapped in greatcoats, their caps pulled down against the bitter wind that blew up the river. Tall masts rose above the heads of the crowd, and the noise of movement, ships loading and unloading, mingled with the screams of gulls. Somewhere in the distance, a church bell rang. It was another world compared to the markets of Bundelkhand.

Dakkar's colourful suit and turban drew many a curious glance. He felt his cheeks redden and he stared down at his hopelessly thin slippers. They had been white once but travelling had greyed them and now brown water seeped through their soles, numbing his already frozen toes. The people here dressed strangely, in knee breeches and socks and long jackets with ridiculously large cuffs.

A face suddenly appeared from the seething crowd. Stern brown eyes glowering above a scarf that smothered the mouth and chin.

'Prince Dakkar, you must come with me immediately,' the man said, towering over the boy. 'Your life is in danger.'

'M-my life?' Dakkar stuttered. 'Ow! You're hurting my arm! Nobody touches the royal personage!'

The man softened his grip on Dakkar's upper arm. 'Forgive me, your highness,' he said, glancing behind him. 'But it is imperative that we get away from here – now!'

Dakkar followed his gaze. Two hawk-faced men with long drooping moustaches and cold eyes weaved in and out of the travellers towards them.

'Those men mean you harm – they are enemies of your father,' hissed the man, pulling at Dakkar. 'You must come with me.'

'This is outrageous,' Dakkar spluttered. 'Where are my servants? I don't even know who you are!'

'Your servants are dead, their throats cut by those ruffi-ans,' the man snarled through gritted teeth. He pulled the scarf down, revealing a square jaw and a broad nose. 'I am Count Oginski, your new mentor. Now, are you ready to go or do you want to meet the two thugs over there?'

Oginski didn't wait for an answer but pulled Dakkar into the mass of people and hurried along the quay towards the streets of the city.

Dakkar's heart raced and his knees nearly buckled as he bumped into passing dock workers and ships' passengers. Oginski's grip held firm. Every now and then Dakkar peered back and saw a stern eye or a determined stride through the throng. Once he thought he glimpsed shining steel. *A blade!*

Oginski whisked him into a side alley, nearly dragging Dakkar off his feet.

'Blast! Wrong one,' Oginski said, skidding to a halt and slapping his palms against the brick wall that ended the alley. 'It's a dead end!'

Dakkar stumbled into Oginski, his breathing ragged, tears prickling the back of his eyes. He could smell sweat and the stink of the puddled alleyway. Muffled shouts and footsteps grew nearer and then the two men appeared at the mouth of the passage.

'The boy is ours, Oginski,' one of the men growled, pulling a long blade from his jacket pocket. 'Hand him over and we'll give you a quick death.'

'Come and get him then.' Oginski grinned, crouching and pushing Dakkar to the back of the alley.

The first man lunged but Oginski stepped back and grabbed his arm, twisting it upward with a sickening crack. The other assailant had closed in quickly and raised his own blade high.

Without thinking, Dakkar leapt forward and punched hard with both hands into the man's kidneys. The man gave a hiss of pain and turned on Dakkar.

Snatching the dagger that fell from the first man's

grip, Oginski swung round and buried it in the second attacker's neck. Something wet spattered Dakkar's cheek and jacket. Their opponent fell with a gargling oath and lay still, his blood reddening the pools of mud on the ground.

Dakkar stared at the twitching man and then at his blood-speckled hands. The other assailant lay slumped, groaning and nursing his mangled arm.

'Come quickly,' Oginski said, grabbing Dakkar again. 'There is no time – these men were only the first.'

Again they ran, pushing people aside, ignoring the curses yelled after them as they sent folk stumbling into each other. Left and right, right and left, they clattered on through the smoky streets, until Dakkar became dizzy and gasped for breath.

Suddenly, Oginski stopped, making Dakkar slip into the foul slime that coated the cobbled streets. Oginski gave a whistle and a horse-drawn carriage rumbled from a side street.

'Get in,' Oginski snapped, yanking the door open.

Dakkar clambered up and threw himself down on the wooden bench inside. His head spun and his heart hammered at his ribs. Oginski jumped straight in after him.

'We are safe,' he said, as the carriage began to rattle across the cobbles.

'Thank you,' Dakkar gasped, slumping in the seat.

For a second, the two of them sat panting for breath. Oginski handed Dakkar a handkerchief, pointing to his face. Dakkar wiped and looked in horror at the red stains on the cloth.

'Not yours,' Oginski said, getting his breath back. He smiled and Dakkar grinned back in spite of his shock.

'Who were those men?' Dakkar said after a moment.

'Assassins,' Oginski said, staring through the curtains that covered the windows. 'They could be any number of people. British East India Company, Russians . . . Who else wants your father's kingdom?'

'Many, many people,' Dakkar said, nodding.

'But you are safe now,' Oginski said again, folding his arms. 'So, the great Rajah of Bundelkhand sends his eldest son to Count Oginski for an education. What was wrong with the schools of this land?'

'I don't like school,' Dakkar grumbled. 'I ran away.'

'To run away from your only refuge in a strange land is brave indeed,' Oginski mused, smiling at Dakkar approvingly. 'At the tender age of ten years old too.'

'The scholars were idiots and the masters were buffoons!' Dakkar said, pouting his bottom lip. 'I learned nothing trapped in those stuffy classrooms all day!'

'And what about the previous school, my prince?' Oginski said, raising his eyebrows. 'And the one before that? You've run away from three schools in the last year!'

'No,' Dakkar protested. 'I was expelled from the last school. One of the masters tried to beat me.'

'And?' Oginski said, his smile frozen on his lips.

'I beat *him*,' Dakkar said, suppressing a grin. He leaned forward and reached for the curtains.

Oginski grabbed his shoulder, yanking him back.

'Please, my prince,' he said. 'I need to keep your where-abouts a total secret.'

'I was just going to look out,' Dakkar muttered.

'If you look out and a passing local sees you, with your dark features and jewelled turban, he'll mention it to his friends in the local public house. Soon it will be all over town,' Oginski said, staring into Dakkar's dark eyes. 'It will be only a matter of time before that knowledge falls into the wrong hands.'

Dakkar flung himself back in the seat and folded his arms. Soon the motion of the carriage and the exertion of the chase tipped him into a restless sleep.

Dakkar felt as though he were falling. As he fell through his dream, he heard his father's voice. Dakkar could see his sunken eyes, the long, grey beard barely concealing the pinched cheekbones.

'You are going to learn how to be a leader of men,' his father said. 'You will be taught by the best, by a nobleman who has known our hardships.'

'But he's only ten years old – he's still a child.' His mother's voice echoed across the miles. 'Give him a few years more. Let him enjoy his childhood.'

'He needs to learn how best he can serve his people,' his father spat, anger gleaming in his eyes, 'before he has no people left to serve . . .'

The earth began to shake and a searing pain split through Dakkar's skull. Gradually, he found himself back on the bench in the carriage as it rattled and rolled him around. He felt a familiar tightness in his stomach and pressure in his throat. The sea voyage from India to England had not been kind to him and the memory of it was returning to him now. Oginski sat opposite, watching him.

'Are you all right?' he asked, leaning forward.

Dakkar threw his head down and heaved a watery pool of vomit over Oginski's boots. 'I don't always travel well,' Dakkar gasped, choking back the acid burn in his throat.

'I am sorry to hear that, my prince,' Oginski said, grimacing at his feet and passing Dakkar another handkerchief. 'You'll get used to it. Your new home is close to the sea – we will spend many hours in its company.'

'I hate the sea,' Dakkar groaned, putting the handkerchief to his mouth. 'And I hate learning.'

'You say that now, your highness,' Oginski said, smiling, 'but you will see. My lessons are different.'

He rapped the ceiling with his knuckles and the carriage came to a halt.

'There are fresh clothes in that trunk,' he said, pointing to a large box on the seat beside him. 'I shall step outside while you change.'

Oginski climbed out and Dakkar glimpsed a hedgerow and fields. He opened the trunk and found woollen European clothes.

'And why would I want to wear these ridiculous garments?' Dakkar shouted out to Oginski.

'They're warmer and they don't smell of vomit,' Oginski replied. 'Your highness.'

'Barbarians,' Dakkar muttered, pulling a face. He undressed and dragged them on. They felt strange and uncomfortable – the fabric scratched his skin and the thick material was stiff – but they were warm.

They travelled for days, often in complete silence. At night, they stopped at small taverns or farmsteads, where Oginski paid handsomely for the innkeeper or farmer's silence.

'Speak to no one,' Oginski said.

'That's easy enough,' Dakkar snorted. 'I have nothing to say to them!'

Dakkar slept well enough – the journey and the motion sickness exhausted him. Dakkar wondered if Oginski slept at all though – he seemed on constant alert, his eyes always roaming over their surroundings.

'Where are we going?' Dakkar asked.

'To my castle,' Oginski replied. 'But it's better if you don't know exactly where that is.'

Finally, after days of bumping over potholed tracks, Oginski relaxed and pushed back the curtains. The clatter of the carriage made Dakkar wince but the welcome draught of cold air soothed his aching head somewhat. He stared out across an open moor that was devoid of any landmarks but one. In the distance, the moor ended in an abrupt cliff edge. Evening was falling quickly and, silhouetted starkly against the dying sun, stood a tower, pointing skyward like a witch's finger.

'Welcome, Prince Dakkar of Bundelkhand,' Oginski said. 'Welcome to the castle.'

SOMEWHERE IN CORNWALL, 1814

CHAPTER ONE
DROWNING

I'll never make it, Dakkar thought. *I am going to die.*

The freezing water pressed in on him, seeping into his nose and mouth as he kicked and flailed towards the pale light of the surface. Salt stung his eyes and the thundering of his heart merged with the roar of the tide. The mosaic pattern of the foam on the surface above him seemed so close yet too far to reach. More salt water forced itself into Dakkar's mouth, his lungs burning for oxygen. His limbs felt feeble as he tried to swim faster. The swirling sea darkened, and his vision began to fail.

Then a calmness embraced him. He loved the sea. He loved sitting on the gravelly bed watching wrasse and gurnard weave among the kelp and luminous anemones. It wouldn't be so bad just to slip back down and rest there for ever. No more lessons, no more nagging from Oginski.

But what about Mother and Father? He hadn't seen them in four years – hadn't heard from them, even. Would they ever know he lay lifeless at the bottom of the sea?

The dark shape of a hand plunged through the waves above, startling Dakkar into action again. Fingers tangled themselves in his thick, black hair and pulled. Fiery pain burned through his scalp but the sudden cold as he broke the surface forced him to gulp at the welcome air.

'You must control your breathing while you're at the bottom,' said Oginski, his saviour. 'You waste your breath, you die.'

'Thank you, Oginski,' Dakkar gasped, collapsing on to the rocks on which Oginski squatted. 'I'll remember that next time you try to drown me!'

Dakkar rolled over, still spluttering and coughing. His stomach twisted with pain as he retched up half the ocean. The bright sky dazzled him and the cold breeze prickled his skin. It was a few minutes before he could focus and see Oginski properly.

'How long?' Dakkar panted.

'Six minutes,' Oginski replied. 'But you could stay down for longer if you had faith in yourself.'

The big man stood up and loomed over Dakkar. He was a square block of a man, with greying curly hair, dark brooding eyes. To Dakkar he looked like he had been cut from the very cliffs behind him.

He extended a hand and, when Dakkar took it, nearly pulled him into the air. Dakkar stumbled to his feet and grabbed the thick woollen blanket that Oginski offered him. He wrapped it round his shivering shoulders, revelling in the glow of warmth it provided.

'You . . .' Oginski began, and then stared out to sea.

'What is it?' Dakkar followed his gaze and saw something break the surface.

A seal leapt high out of the water. A huge tentacle snaked up out of the sea, followed by another and another. Dakkar stood dumbstruck as the tentacles wrapped themselves round the seal. The seal gave a hoarse bark then vanished below the surface.

For a second, Oginski stood silent, staring in apparent disbelief at what he had just seen. Then he turned on his heel.

'Quickly,' he snapped. 'We must get back to the castle.'

'But shouldn't we raise the alarm?' Dakkar called, hurrying after his mentor. 'Let the locals know there's something out there?'

'I'm not sure they'd believe us,' Oginski muttered.

'It looked like some kind of giant squid,' Dakkar gasped.

'That's what it looked like,' Oginski replied. 'Whatever it was, it was something bad. Something very bad. Come on.'

Dakkar had been sheltered by the cliff face but now, as they reached the top, a raw wind cut into him despite the woollen blanket. He shivered and huddled into the warm fabric. Across the flat cliff top stood the castle. It looked bleaker than ever to Dakkar.

'I'm not sure what to do, Dakkar,' Oginski said with a shrug.

'We *m-must* warn the village,' Dakkar stammered through chattering teeth. 'Imagine if that had been a fisherman, not a seal!'

Oginski stopped and turned to look at Dakkar. A smile cracked the man's stony face as he laid a hand on Dakkar's shoulder.

'You're a good lad, Dakkar,' Oginski said. 'Your concern for others does you great credit.'

Dakkar felt some warmth despite the wind and the fact that he wore only a bathing suit. *To think I used to fear this man*, Dakkar thought, remembering his first night at the castle. *But I was only ten years old.*

It wasn't really a castle, more of a tower built on the cliff edge. Oginski had rebuilt it from ancient medieval ruins. The tower loomed above them, black and full of foreboding. It was round, stretching high above, with a conical roof of slate. A few cottages and outhouses huddled at its base. Thick glass and shutters protected the square windows that dotted the smooth stone face of it.

'More surprises!' Dakkar said as his gaze fell to the huge front door. Two horses stood outside, damp and dejected, in front of a black carriage. 'We have visitors!'

Oginski's face darkened. In the four years Dakkar had been at the castle, he could count the number of visitors on one hand. They hurried past the carriage, where a surly driver in red military uniform was waiting. He stood to attention but Oginski merely gave a grunt and hurled himself at the oak front door. Dakkar hurried after.

In the wood-panelled hall, Mrs Evans, the housekeeper,

bobbed and fussed, her black ringlets quivering under her white mob cap. She reminded Dakkar of a plump blackbird.

'Count Oginski,' she said breathlessly. 'Forgive me, sir, I know how particular you are about visitors but he insisted. I put him in your study.' She handed Oginski the visitor's card.

Oginski glanced at it, snorted and threw it to the floor. He turned and strode into the study, slamming the door behind him before Dakkar could see the man inside.

Dakkar grabbed the card. 'Commander Blizzard,' he read aloud. 'His Majesty's Navy.'

He dashed back outside and crept close to the study window, peering in.

Oginski sat at his desk, his broad shoulders and thick arms making the furniture look like flimsy toys. His square face was stern. His deep brow cast shadows over his eyes as he sat opposite a young gentleman dressed in black – black jacket, black breeches and stockings. His hair shone golden at the top of this dark garb, giving him a pale and sickly appearance. A thin scar trickled down his left cheek from the corner of his eye to his chin, making one half of his face sad and mournful. A naval man, Dakkar thought. That might explain the scar but he doesn't look like any kind of sailor I know.

Ignoring the cold, Dakkar pressed his ear to the thin glass and listened.

'Let's cut the pleasantries. When Commander Blizzard knocks at your door,' Oginski said, his face flat and unsmiling, 'he has either come to arrest you or to ask for a favour. And as I've committed no crime . . .'

'No?' Blizzard smiled, raising his eyebrows.

'No,' Oginski growled back, holding Blizzard's gaze.

Dakkar frowned. *Is Blizzard going to arrest him?*

'There are rumours surrounding this castle, Count Oginski,' Blizzard said, a chill smile set on his face. 'Strange noises in the night. Lights visible from the sea. Unusual deliveries . . .'

'Idle gossip,' Oginski snorted, waving a dismissive hand. 'The local fisherfolk are always looking for a tale to tell in the local tavern.'

'That may be but often rumours have a basis in truth. I'll cut to the chase, sir,' Blizzard said, breaking eye contact with Oginski. 'The Americans have built a weapon. We want you to join us in a mission to destroy it.'

'You refer, of course, to Fulton's Floating Steam Battery,' Oginski said, giving a fleeting smirk at the pale gentleman's consternation. He rose from his seat and poured two glasses of port from a decanter on his desk.

'How on earth do you know about that?' Blizzard gasped, taking the glass in a limp hand.

'Do you really think the construction of a steam-powered ship capable of carrying sixteen thirty-two-pound guns would escape my notice?' Oginski sneered. 'I am a man of science, Blizzard, and an engineer.'

'The best in the world, some say.' Blizzard nodded. 'Although you've never made such a ship for us.'

A steam warship, Dakkar thought, clenching his fists with excitement. *How I'd love to see that!*

'Why are you so worried?' Oginski continued, ignoring Blizzard's comment. 'The thing isn't fit for the high seas. At best, it's suitable for defending shipyards and bays. It's not as if the Americans are going to sail up the Thames in it.'

'Not yet,' Blizzard muttered, and seemed to go a shade paler – if that were possible. 'But once they perfect the hull Britain's mastery of the seas may be a thing of the past.'

Dakkar noticed Oginski grimace and incline his head. 'Would that be a bad thing?'

'Of course,' Blizzard hissed. His blue eyes were icy. 'It puzzles me, sir, that, despite your immense talent and intellect, you've never invented any weapon that we could use in this great nation's defence. If I doubted your loyalty to the government that shelters you . . .'

'My loyalty is not in doubt, sir,' Oginski said, shaking his head. 'It's just that I see no need for me to accompany you to America. Why can't you destroy this vessel yourselves?'

'We aren't entirely sure of its capabilities,' Blizzard replied. 'Your knowledge of engineering and design would prove invaluable.'

'The answer is still no,' Oginski said.

'Is it your friendship with Robert Fulton, the designer of the ship, that stops you?' the commander asked stiffly.

Now it was Oginski's turn to look shocked. He recovered himself quickly. 'Of course not!' he said, giving a brittle laugh. 'I haven't seen Fulton for many years and

I'm even less likely to now that America and Britain are at war!'

'Indeed, we *are* at war, sir,' Blizzard said. 'And if I thought you were in any way colluding with the Americans . . .'

'The very suggestion is insulting, sir,' Oginski said, his voice so low that Dakkar could barely hear it through the glass. 'I have nothing to hide.'

'Good,' Blizzard said, placing the port glass on Oginski's desk. 'Then either you agree to help me or I'll search this tower from top to bottom and report anything suspicious.'

'You can do what you like,' Oginski spat.

'Yes,' Blizzard said, a grin twisting his pale face. 'I can.' He paused at the door. 'My ship is in Fullacombe Harbour if you change your mind. Tomorrow evening we sail for America with or without you. A troop of my marines will visit you shortly before we leave. Be ready.'

Dakkar crouched down below the window and watched as Blizzard strode out of the house. The pale man paused before climbing into his carriage and looked straight at Dakkar, who was still wrapped in the blanket.

'Your highness,' Blizzard said, raising his hat and giving another grin.

The carriage clattered away from the house, leaving Dakkar staring after it.

CHAPTER TWO

THE STRANGER IN THE TAVERN

Oginski charged across the castle hall, papers clutched in his fist. He stopped and grabbed Dakkar by his lapels.

'He called you "your highness?"' Oginski said, staring deep into Dakkar's eyes. 'You're certain?'

'Yes, Oginski,' Dakkar replied. 'Why are you so worried?'

'I've told you before. Your father has many enemies,' Oginski said, stuffing the papers into a leather bag. 'He specifically requested that your location and identity be kept secret.'

'So you say,' Dakkar muttered.

Oginski stopped wrestling with the bag and looked at Dakkar. 'And what's that supposed to mean?' he demanded.

'If my father has so many enemies,' Dakkar said, not meeting Oginski's eye, 'how will I fight them? I'm not learning the art of war here. Strategy, commanding troops – these are the things I need to learn. Yet you teach me how to swim, to build canals, to design machines.'

'A great leader doesn't just fight for his people – he cares for his people,' Oginski sighed. 'Do your people love your father or fear him? Do they have irrigation for their crops? Do they have steam engines to pump flood water out of their mines, to pull their loads?'

'No, Oginski, but –'

'I teach you the skills you need to build a modern, enlightened country,' Oginski snapped, pulling his bag shut. 'If you want to learn how to fight, then join the army. Afterwards, if you don't die in one of Europe's insane wars, you'll be able to go home and die fighting there.'

'I only meant –'

'I don't have time for this argument, Dakkar,' Oginski said, striding for the door. 'I'm going to Fullacombe to hear what rumours are circulating. I'll be back this evening. In the meantime, stay inside. Don't swim and don't talk to anyone except the staff.'

Before Dakkar could reply, Oginski banged the door shut behind him.

Dakkar scowled at the door, arms folded tight against his chest. Mrs Evans laid a hand on his arm.

'Come on now, Dakkar, dear,' she whispered. 'Come and have a piece of cake and some tea. You'll feel better then.'

Dakkar allowed himself to be led away to the kitchen, where Mrs Evans sat him down at the scrubbed table.

'It's not fair, Mrs Evans,' Dakkar said, sniffing. 'I'm a young man now and yet Oginski treats me like a child!'

'The count has always been a secretive man,' Mrs Evans said, cutting into the thick fruit cake. 'He's the same with everyone. Folk around here don't have much time for him. He never gives a "good mornin'" or a smile to strangers. He's been worse lately, spending even more time down in his cellar.'

Dakkar nodded. Oginski had been spending so long down there recently that Dakkar had wondered what he was up to. Usually Oginski shared his projects and presented them to Dakkar as learning opportunities – together they'd built a pump for the local mine and fixed the clock in the church tower.

'He's always so nervous and agitated,' Dakkar mumbled through a mouthful of sweet crumbs. 'Like when I first met him.'

'You led him a merry dance then,' Mrs Evans chuckled. 'Pardon me for saying so, Dakkar, but you were a little monster. You ran away five times, no less, clamberin' out of windows, hiding in the coal shed . . .'

A grin spread across Dakkar's face. 'I wasn't that bad, was I?'

'We weren't expectin' you, see?' Mrs Evans laughed. 'When the count first brought you home, we thought he'd found a faery changeling on the road!'

'But the way he changed this morning when he –' Dakkar dropped his cake slice on to the table and jumped to his feet. 'The squid, in the water. I forgot!'

'What are you on about, lad?' Mrs Evans said as Dakkar hurried out of the kitchen. 'Here, come back! Where are you going? Count Oginski said you weren't to leave the castle!'

Dakkar rushed into the hall and through the front door. Out across the flat cliff path he ran, muttering and cursing as he did. The grey, rain-filled clouds hadn't broken and Dakkar could see the little village huddled around the river outlet where the cliffs sloped down to the sea. The stones crunched under his feet and the nettles that fringed the path whipped at his hands and legs, but he didn't slow.

I've got to warn them about the thing in the sea, he thought. *If someone died, I'd never forgive myself.*

Soon the low cottages came into view and Dakkar was in the heart of the village. He hurried to the tavern and crashed against the door, tumbling inside. The hard tiles stung his knees and the smell of beer and tobacco smoke tickled his nose. A fire crackled in the hearth and scrubbed wooden tables and chairs filled the small room. A couple of toothless old men with leather-brown skin and matted white beards sat in the corner by the fire.

The taverner's wife gave a squeal and slopped beer from the mugs she held.

'What on earth are you playin' at?' she screeched, slamming the drinks down on the table.

'I'm sorry,' Dakkar panted, scrambling to his feet. 'But I had to warn you.'

'Warn? What about?' one of the old men piped up in the corner.

'I saw something,' Dakkar gasped, slowly getting his breath back. 'It was in the sea this morning.'

'You're the boy from the castle, ain't you?' the taverner's wife said, narrowing her eyes.

'Yes. My name is Dakkar,' he said, rubbing his forehead. 'You must listen.'

A chair leg scraped along the tiled floor and Dakkar turned at the sound, peering into the shadows.

A squat, hunchbacked man, with small, glittering eyes stood leering at him. One hand rested on the table, supporting him as he leaned forward. Dakkar could see that his middle and index fingers were missing. His wide mouth split into a grin that was too full of brown tombstone teeth.

Dakkar gave a gasp, trying not to stare at the man's blistered, scarred skin and mutilated hands.

'Well, Dakkar, you ain't welcome here,' the taverner's wife said, wiping her hands on her apron and glancing at the man in the shadows. 'Go on, get back home!'

'But there's something out there in the sea!' Dakkar persisted. 'It could be dangerous.'

The squat man shuffled forward and gave a sniff, and his grin widened.

'Lots of fish, I shouldn't doubt,' one of the old men cackled.

'Go on, shoo!' the taverner's wife snapped, and she bundled Dakkar out through the door.

Dakkar didn't resist – the strange man disturbed him. It wasn't so much his appearance as the look he had given

Dakkar. Full of menace. Glancing back, he saw the man peering at him through the tavern's small leaded window.

At least he'd warned the villagers. He couldn't do any more. Dakkar ran back towards the castle, the wind battering him. Dakkar couldn't help checking behind him. *Stupid! As if the man would follow me!* Still, all the way home, he couldn't shake the feeling he was being watched.

At last he reached the castle and slammed the heavy door behind him. Silence hung over the hallway as Dakkar scanned the oak panels, the suits of armour standing to attention, the stairs spiralling up to the next floor. He was just opening his mouth to shout for Mrs Evans when something caught his attention.

The cellar door was ajar. Located just under the staircase, it normally stood locked and flush to the varnished panels, almost invisible. Now Dakkar could see the edge of the door and the lock. Oginski must have left it open in his hurry.

Holding his breath, Dakkar tiptoed over to the door and peered down the short flight of steps. An oil lamp glowed dimly but there was no sound of movement. Slowly, he crept down, pressing himself against the wall.

The steps opened into a small room with a workbench, a number of cupboards and some tools scattered on the surfaces. A bookcase filled one wall. Dakkar sneaked up to the workbench and picked up a hammer that lay there. It felt heavy in his hand. He glanced up and what he saw made him gasp.

Pinned to the wall was a drawing of a boat. It was a strange boat, with a covered top and a wheel at the stern, rather like a paddle steamer. Written in neat copperplate above it were the words *Oginski's Patent Undersea Submersible*.

An underwater boat! Dakkar thought, running his fingers over the lines on the plan.

He read the legend under the diagram: *Ballast tanks within hull for submerging* . . .

For some time, Dakkar stood, lost in the design of the craft. *So this is what Oginski has been so secretive about! But he couldn't have spent all this time just drawing up this plan – maybe he's actually making it!*

Looking about, Dakkar could see a riveted metal door in the wall opposite. He pulled it open, wincing as it squealed on its hinges. This entrance opened on to a long flight of shallow steps. Through it Dakkar could smell the sea and hear the distant waves rolling against the cliffs. Pulling the door closed behind him, he took the first step and immediately slipped on the slimy green seaweed that coated everything. Dakkar's backside went numb as he bumped down every step. He could feel the damp from the steps soaking through his trousers. Finally, he reached the last step and staggered to his feet, groaning and rubbing his aching bottom.

He looked up at the huge sea cavern in which he stood, his eyes widening in amazement. It towered above him, echoing with the roar of the tide. High above his head, daylight streamed through a hole punched in the ceiling.

He stood on a platform of rock that rose above a natural pool. Somewhere below, he supposed, the sea had bored its way in through a seam of softer rock, making a tunnel.

But what really caught Dakkar's attention was the strange craft that bobbed in the centre of the pool, tied in place by strong ropes. It reminded him of a cocoon. The deck was flat at the back and held what looked like a wheel from a watermill or a paddle from a miniature paddle steamer. Portholes lined the sides of the 'lid' and the hull of the boat.

'The submersible,' Dakkar whispered.

A plank bridged the gap from the rocky plateau to the craft. Dakkar tiptoed along it and, leaning forward, he pressed his palms on the polished wooden hull. As he did so, his knuckles grazed a brass lever. Without thinking, he pulled at it and scrambled back as the lid lifted with a hiss.

The submersible was open.

Two cushioned seats occupied the front of the craft. Dakkar could see the captain's seat, inviting him to climb in. *What harm would it do just to sit inside?* He stretched a leg into the craft.

CHAPTER THREE
THE *MAKARA*

Dakkar sat in the boat and ran his hands over the wheel in front of him. He poked the black substance that ran along the edge of the lid.

'Rubber from the Americas,' he muttered to himself. 'It must form a waterproof seal when the top is shut.'

A memory of Oginski melting rubber in a pan in the kitchen came to mind. Mrs Evans had gone mad and the smell had made Dakkar sick to his stomach.

'This could be the best waterproofing for ships ever,' Oginski had said.

'It'll be the death of me, Count Oginski,' Mrs Evans had snapped back, pushing him out of her kitchen, shaking her head at her ruined pots and pans.

Dakkar looked behind him at the engine that filled half the craft. A central wheel with thick teeth sat in the midst of a mass of cogs and springs. Wires and tubes spiralled off around the inside of the craft, disappearing into parts of the hull and the control panel at the front. In the middle of this sat a box with a crank handle sticking out of it.

'Surely it isn't clockwork!' Dakkar said, climbing out of his seat.

He heaved at the crank handle. It clicked noisily. Dakkar was panting by the time he felt he could wind no more.

'It's amazing,' he whispered, staring at the complex mass of cogs and springs. *It must have some incredible gear system to generate enough power to move. I wonder how often it needs to be wound.*

Steadying himself as the craft rocked on the water, Dakkar eased himself back into his seat and gripped the small ship's wheel that poked out in front of him. Several levers and taps dotted the smooth wooden panel behind the wheel.

Dakkar closed his eyes and thought of the plan he'd seen in the cellar. The boat's hull had two layers and a compartment between them could fill with water and submerge the craft. He reached for the lid, then stopped and bit his lip. He wanted to plunge underwater to see how deep the boat could go. *But Oginski will go berserk if he finds out! If he finds out!* Dakkar thought. *But he doesn't have to. He has his secrets, so I'll have mine!*

The submersible felt cramped and stifling as Dakkar pulled the lid down and secured the watertight seal with a lever. Thinking back to the plan, Dakkar twirled a brass disc at the centre of the main wheel and the engine clanked into life, making the hairs on the back of his neck prickle.

The craft didn't move.

Dakkar frowned, his heart thumping. He glanced around and noticed a brass handle in among the levers behind the wheel. He whirled it round and heard a gurgling sound as seawater filled the hull of the craft. Gradually, the waterline crept halfway over the portholes, but there it stopped. *What's going on?* Dakkar wondered.

It was then that he noticed the tight line of rope stretching to the side of the cavern. He laughed to himself. *I forgot to untie her!*

Dakkar whirled the handle back, relieved to hear the bubbling gush of water as the hull filled with air once more and the boat floated to the surface. Quickly, he opened the lid and scrambled out, almost falling into the pool as he hurried to untie the ropes that held the craft fast.

Then he sat back in the captain's seat, secured the lid and whirled the submerging handle again. The craft pitched and rolled alarmingly and his ears popped as it began to sink. Bubbles and foam seethed around the portholes as they submerged but, gradually, a misty, blue landscape of rocks and swaying seaweed was revealed.

'Astonishing,' Dakkar murmured, staring out at the shoals of fish and the anemones clinging to the jagged rocks. In the distance, a dark opening scarred the wall of the cavern and the seaweed showed that the sea did indeed come in through there.

For some time Dakkar sat transfixed by the view through the portholes. Then, shaking himself, he scanned the controls.

A brass lever sat in a slot engraved with commands such as *Full Ahead*, *Slow*, *Backwater* and *Stop*. He pushed the lever forward to *Full Ahead* and the engine behind him whirred as the craft began to slide forward. Dakkar's heart raced as the submersible's speed increased. As it went faster, the cavern began to flash past him.

Dakkar pulled at the wheel, sending the craft lurching to one side and banging his head. In a panic, Dakkar twirled the wheel the other way, trying to correct the sudden turn. A huge pinnacle of barnacled stone loomed ahead.

With a yelp, Dakkar yanked the wheel towards him and the sudden upward tilt threw him back in his seat. The surface boiled above as the craft careered up the face of the rock. A wet slapping sound of weed hitting the hull told him how close he was to tearing the body of the craft against the rough stone. Dakkar's mouth felt dry and sweat trickled down his back as he fumbled for the lever and dragged it to *Stop*. The craft came to rest and righted itself. The engine's whine died to a muted tick, barely heard over Dakkar's anxious panting.

A smile forced itself across Dakkar's face, followed by a chuckle, and then he gave a whoop and punched the air, banging his knuckles on the roof.

'That was incredible!' he shouted, almost deafening himself in the small confines of the boat.

Oginski's Patent Undersea Submersible, he mused.
O.P.U.S. Not a bad name. But I'll call you the Makara,
after the sea serpent ridden by Varuna, god of the ocean!

Once more he spun the submerging wheel and the
engine blasted the water from the hollow hull of the
newly christened *Makara*. Bubbles obscured the view and
Dakkar's stomach lurched as the *Makara* bobbed up to the
surface.

Carefully, he guided her to the side of the pool and
pulled the lever. The lid sprang up and Dakkar stiffened,
suppressing a gasp.

Oginski stood glaring at him, hands on hips, his face a
mask of anger.

CHAPTER FOUR
NIGHTMARES

Dakkar hunched his shoulders and looked at his feet as he stepped out of the *Makara*. 'I'm sorry, Oginski. I didn't mean to –'

'I turn my back for a few hours and you go sneaking into my workshop?' Oginski said, his voice trembling with rage.

'The cellar door was open. I saw the plans of the *Makara* and –' Dakkar began.

'The what?' Oginski cut in, his eyes cold and narrow.

'The *Makara*,' Dakkar mumbled, his cheeks flushed. 'That's what I call her. She's incredible –'

'What's incredible is that you didn't drown yourself!' Oginski spat. 'It was a foolish and idiotic thing to do!'

Oginski marched Dakkar up the steps. It was all Dakkar could do to keep from slipping again. Tears stung his eyes. He felt once more like the ten-year-old who arrived at the castle.

'You are to forget everything you saw today,' Oginski snapped, pushing Dakkar into his bedroom. 'The . . . the *Makara*, as you call her, is a prototype, and a pretty poor one at that. I'll be scrapping her tomorrow.'

'But, Oginski –'

'As for *you*,' Oginski interrupted again. 'You can stay here without supper and think about how you can persuade me to trust you ever again!'

The door slammed and Dakkar heard the key turn in the lock. Dakkar hurled a pillow at it.

'It's not fair!' he shouted. 'Maybe if you had trusted me then I wouldn't have been tempted to take her!'

The door remained locked and Oginski's footsteps slowly faded down the hall.

'I hate you!' Dakkar bellowed, punching the remaining pillows and choking back the sobs.

Gradually, he stilled, grumbling until an uneasy sleep overcame him.

In his dreams, Dakkar was back in Bundelkhand, in perfumed palaces of carved marble fountains and silk cushions. He was hiding behind a thick silk curtain, spying. A huge black cobra swayed in front of his father.

'My son grows soft,' the rajah said to the snake. 'His mother spoils him with treats. He does not see the difficulties of ruling an ungrateful mob.'

'He is bright and ssstrong,' hissed the cobra. 'A keeeen learner and fassst.'

'He spends too long in the classroom,' his father murmured. 'He should go out into the world. Learn to fight our enemies.'

'Give him to me,' hissed the cobra, swishing back and forth hypnotically. 'I will make a fearsssome leader out of him. He will crush his enemies and demand the respect of hisss people.'

'Dakkar!' his father yelled. 'Come out!'

'Give him to meeee.' The snake rose up and slithered around Dakkar's feet, binding his legs. 'Give him to meeee.'

The cobra seemed to grow and twist round Dakkar's body, round his neck. Dry scaly skin enveloped his face, smothering him, plunging him into blackness. He couldn't see; he couldn't breathe. He tried to scream but his mouth was sealed.

Dakkar sat bolt upright, yelling. His bedclothes were soaked in sweat and yet he shivered. The screaming continued but it wasn't him.

It was coming from downstairs.

Dakkar shook his head and rubbed his eyes. The grey of dawn trickled through the thick curtains. He could hear shouting, banging and clattering.

'Oginski?' Dakkar croaked, easing himself off the bed on to the cold floorboards. 'Mrs Evans?'

Something crashed to the floor downstairs.

The door was still locked. Dakkar could see the key in the lock. Ripping the picture of the sea anemone he'd been drawing from the easel, Dakkar slid it under the door and thumped the keyhole from his side. The key clinked on to the paper. Dakkar gently pulled the paper back under the door, bringing the key with it. His fingers trembled as he fumbled with the lock.

Pushing the door open, Dakkar stumbled down the stairs. Broken glass and splintered furniture littered the hallway. The suits of armour that had always stood sentry were broken and scattered.

A tall, thin figure stood in the doorframe. With his hands he held Mrs Evans by the throat. Her lifeless eyes stared at the ceiling.

'Ah, Prince Dakkar,' the figure whispered, reminding Dakkar of the snake in his nightmare. 'I was just . . . making enquiries as to your whereabouts but this lady seems to have died. Most inconvenient!'

'Dakkar, run!' Oginski appeared in the doorway, held by two burly figures shrouded in long black robes. 'The *Makara*!'

One of the shrouded figures brought a fist down on the back of Oginski's neck, sending him to the ground, senseless.

'Take Oginski to the ship,' the dark figure said, and pointed a finger at Dakkar. 'Get the boy too.'

Dakkar leapt down the last three steps and landed at the foot of the stairs. The cellar door stood ajar again. The dark figure loomed above him and Dakkar threw his gaze back to Oginski, trying not to look at the slumped form of Mrs Evans.

'Yes, run, Prince Dakkar, run,' the figure laughed. 'See how far you get!'

The scarred, hunched man from the tavern appeared from behind the dark figure and lunged at Dakkar.

With a yell, Dakkar scurried across the hall and through the cellar door, slamming it shut. Scrabbling with the bolt, he managed to slam it home just as someone crunched against the door.

A heavy thump echoed around the cellar, but Dakkar didn't stop. He rushed into the dank room and through the iron door. Forgetting the worn, slippery steps, Dakkar staggered and fell flat on to his back, sliding down towards the pool. Every step battered his ribs, forcing the air from his lungs. Cold slime chilled his bare legs and his nightshirt rode up under his armpits, binding his arms, making recovery impossible.

Gasping for breath, he stopped at the bottom and, groaning, sat up. The hammering at the metal door above him stopped abruptly. Only his panting breath, echoing around the high roof of the cavern, and the suck and slosh of the tide could be heard. Dakkar frowned. *Have they given up?*

Pulling himself to his feet, Dakkar glanced up the steps and then quickly turned back to face the pool. Something else was here with him.

A bony click accompanied the appearance of a long, stick-like leg from the water. Then another leg, and another, followed by a blue, spiny boulder with two black, beady eyes on stalks and mandibles that fanned the air. It was a massive crab. It rose up above Dakkar on its long spidery legs, clicking sharp pincers at him.

Choking down a scream, Dakkar threw himself back as the pincers whistled through the air, inches from his face. He landed on the steps behind him with a gasp. The crab scuttled forward, the points of its legs clicking loudly in the cave. Again, it stabbed with its pincers, slashing viciously through thin air as Dakkar scrabbled up the steps backward.

The crab scurried up the first few steps, scraping at the slick rock as it tried to get a grip. Seeing his chance, Dakkar lashed out with his feet, kicking its nearest legs. The crab slid down the steps and Dakkar rushed forward, leaping on top of its carapace. Claws snapped at him as he scrambled up and behind the creature, landing close to the *Makara*.

Dakkar's fingers felt numb as he fumbled with the rope that held the boat, desperately trying to untie it. The crab had spun round now and scurried towards him again. Its claws grazed Dakkar's leg as he threw himself to the other side of the *Makara* and untied the final rope.

Clinging to the top of the boat, Dakkar kicked out with one leg and sent the *Makara* drifting away from the edge of the pool. The crab, three of its legs on the boat, straddled the gap. Dakkar rocked, tipping the boat violently and nearly sending himself into the water. The crab scrabbled at the boat and the rocky ledge, trying to keep balanced. Gripping tightly to the rings that studded the *Makara*, Dakkar gave her another roll. This time the crab slipped sideways into the water with a splash that soaked Dakkar.

Without hesitating, he reached down and popped the handle that opened the craft. He slid inside, panting for breath as he slammed the lid down.

Something grated along the bottom of the *Makara*, reverberating through the entire hull. Dakkar shuddered as spiny legs grappled around the *Makara*, scratching against the portholes. The crab clung, upside down, from the hull.

He turned the starter disc in the centre of the wheel and slammed the brass lever to *Backwater*. The engine behind him began to click and whirr. Slowly, the *Makara* eased backward, but the weight of the monstrous passenger slowed her down.

'Right,' Dakkar hissed. 'Let's see how you enjoy this!'

He turned the ballast wheel, shrouding the *Makara* in bubbles, and it sank like a stone. The impact jarred Dakkar out of his seat as the ship rolled on top of the crab. Blood clouded the water, but Dakkar could just make out the creature's legs floating free from the craft.

For a moment, Dakkar sat still, trying to slow his breathing and collect his wits. He sobbed as he thought of what had happened and all that he'd seen. Then he gave a scream as something whacked against the glass of the porthole nearest to him.

Dakkar's scalp prickled at what he saw.

The crab's blood still formed a dark red mist that obscured his view but he could make out a hand pressed against the glass. A large hand, the fingers gnarled and scaly. A thin film of webbed skin stretched between each finger. Another hand slammed against the window on Dakkar's right, making him wince and whimper.

And this time a face peered in through the glass. Marbled, white eyes. A slit of a nose, and Dakkar had the impression of gills fanning the water behind an angular, scaly jaw. Dakkar would have said it was a fish but it looked too human.

More hands slapped at the portholes and thumped the body of the *Makara*. Whatever these creatures were, they were trying to get in.

CHAPTER FIVE

THE INGENIOUS TUNNEL

Gasping for breath and trying not to think of what might be outside, Dakkar scanned the inside of the *Makara* in search of something that might be used as a weapon.

Another thud shook the *Makara*. Dakkar saw a small crank handle and a red button set into a brass plate in the roof of the craft. A small label dangled from it, bearing the symbol of a skull and the words *Use only in emergency. Turn twenty times and press.*

Grabbing the handle, Dakkar jagged it round and round. The hammering outside grew more intense. The planks that formed the hull seemed to be shaking even more . . . *Eighteen, nineteen, twenty.* Dakkar stabbed his thumb into the red button.

A loud bang accompanied a blinding flash of blue lightning that illuminated the whole cavern pool. Shadowy semi-human forms flew back from the craft. Dakkar could see them floating face down in the water.

Electricity, Dakkar thought. Oginski had shown him a friction machine a few months ago – a wheel that you turned and it produced sparks. Dakkar had touched it and yelped as the charge numbed his finger to the knuckle. He smiled fleetingly at the memory. Then frowned at the strange, murky shapes that floated outside. *I must have electrocuted them.*

Dakkar looked back inside the *Makara. It was lucky the handle was labelled.* He stopped and frowned. Every device had a label tied to it. He hadn't noticed before. *Why did Oginski do that?*

A letter lay on the seat next to him. Dakkar picked it up and read it.

Dakkar,

If you are reading this, then my fears have been realised. You are in great danger but you can use the submersible that you christened the Makara to escape. You are a clever lad and will work out her controls.

There is much I would like to tell you but I haven't the time and, for some of those things, I need to look you in the eye and hope you give me the chance to explain. Maybe we'll meet again but I fear that may not be so. Return to your father if you can, and live a good life.

Your mentor,
Oginski

Tears stung Dakkar's eyes. He gave a great gulping sigh. Oginski had known something was going on. That's why he had been so preoccupied and angry.

A distant *boom* vibrated through the water, snapping Dakkar to his senses. The intruders from above were trying to get through the cellar door again. Turning the *Makara* round, Dakkar peered through the porthole, searching for the underwater tunnel he'd spotted when he first submerged yesterday.

Seaweed rippled to and fro at the jagged tunnel entrance. It made Dakkar think of a sleeping sea giant's mouth, the fronds of his beard waving back and forth as he breathed in and out.

Bracing himself, Dakkar pushed the lever to *Full Ahead*, thrilling at the whirr of the engine and the sudden acceleration. The *Makara* shuddered, slowing a little as she hit the current spewing out of the tunnel. Then the tide sucked the water from the pool, dragging the *Makara* through into the darkness. Dakkar winced as the sides of the hull rattled against rock. He wrestled with the wheel to keep the boat steady but the scraping grew louder. Suddenly, the current changed and Dakkar flew forward against the wheel as the tunnel spat the *Makara* back out into the pool.

Another muffled thump told Dakkar that the metal door above was about to give way. He didn't have time to battle with the tide.

Panting, Dakkar climbed out of the seat and wound the engine handle tight. Then he climbed back in and pushed the lever to full power again. Water bubbled around the portholes and Dakkar was pressed into his seat as the tunnel mouth rushed closer. Again the current sucked the *Makara* back in. He fixed his eyes on the centre of the black void, hoping to keep clear of the edges. A thud reverberated through the boat, followed by an ominous screeching of stone on polished planking. Dakkar adjusted the speed as the tunnel wall dashed past him. Then, yet again, the current changed, sending the *Makara* hurtling backward. It clipped the mouth of the tunnel as it did so and went spinning back into the pool.

Dakkar thumped the wheel in frustration. *The* Makara *just doesn't have the power to escape the tide! Why would Oginski build such a marvellous ship in here if he knew she would be stuck?*

'He wouldn't,' Dakkar said aloud. The one thing he knew about Oginski after four years of learning by his side was that the man was a perfectionist. 'So there must be another way out.'

Dakkar steered the *Makara* along the edge of the pool. Fish flitted out of the way and sea anemones fringed the water.

'There!' Dakkar whispered. On the other side of the pool, long fronds of what looked like seaweed obscured another hole in the wall.

As he came closer, Dakkar saw that the fronds were strands of cloth and leather, covering a gap that was too square to be natural but only just big enough for the *Makara* to fit through.

Another *boom* and a crash vibrated through the water, alerting Dakkar that the iron door had given way. There was no time to worry about the size of the entrance or the speed he was going. Dakkar sent the *Makara* full ahead, and the fronds of false seaweed smacked the portholes and brushed along the top of the boat. Then she stopped dead, sending him hurtling against the wheel. Pain lanced through his cheek and chin, and the metallic taste of blood filled his mouth.

Dakkar sat back, wincing as he touched his split lip. The *Makara* was still moving forward! The hum of the engine inside had stopped though, and now Dakkar could hear the clank of ratchets on the outside. The boat shook as it was dragged along some kind of track fixed to either side of the cavern wall.

A clanging noise came from behind the boat and Dakkar watched through the portholes as the water level fell. The *Makara* juddered some way along the track and then came to a halt. Dakkar stared out on to another huge cavern, lit from above by a shaft of daylight. He frowned and pressed his bruised face to the porthole glass. The *Makara* rested on a rounded wooden platform.

Another mechanical clunk made Dakkar start. The *Makara* began to sink into the platform. Dakkar tried to pop the lid but the lever held fast. He looked out again as the sinking stopped with another loud thud.

His fingers sweaty and slippery, Dakkar heaved at the lever to open the lid. He scanned the roof and sides of the boat for any clue as to what was happening. Would he be trapped in here, left to slowly suffocate or starve?

He frowned. Flush to the floor of the *Makara*, behind

the seats, lay a brass hatch lid. Two handles fitted snugly into recesses cut into the lid. Dakkar pulled them up and turned the lid clockwise. With a hiss, the lid came up and Dakkar stared down in amazement.

Beneath him, a ladder ran down into a room very much like the inside of the *Makara*. It was like being inside a giant barrel that lay on its side. Brass bands held polished wooden planks in place. Everything fitted together so closely that Dakkar saw it was all watertight. A chair and a small bed stood in one corner next to a table and a map cupboard. Crates of supplies and skins of water hung from the curved walls of the room. It seemed that the *Makara* had been lowered into a bigger version of herself.

Dakkar slid down the ladder and ran to the huge portholes at the front of the larger craft. The sea sloshed against the larger *Makara*, waves breaking over a pointed nose encased in metal. It was facing towards an opening in the cavern wall across a lagoon of water.

Turning round, Dakkar noticed a large crank handle in the centre of the back wall of this larger vessel. He estimated that this lower room only took up two thirds of the craft. *The rest must be the engine*, he thought. He ran across and tried to turn the handle. It didn't move. It was wound tight and ready to go.

'I wonder,' Dakkar said aloud, and climbed back up into the smaller craft. 'The two *Makara*s must fit together, the small one controlling the larger one.' Dakkar tried to imagine the gears and cogs turning in the back of the larger craft but his head still throbbed from banging it before.

Settling into the seat, he pushed the lever to *Full Ahead*. Behind him, the engine began to whirr and click. Below, a clanking sound grew into a deafening rattle and then a hum as the *Makara* surged forward.

Dakkar had never moved so fast. The cavern walls, stalagmites and white foam flashed by. Then clear daylight streamed in through the portholes, dazzling Dakkar for a moment. He spun the submerging wheel and gave a yell of joy as the *Makara* plunged into the waves of the open sea in a confusion of spray and bubbles.

For a moment, he forgot the horrific events of that morning: Oginski's cries, poor Mrs Evans, the crab and the strange fish-men. Only the foam and the water rushing past existed, the silver shoals of fish swirling out of the way. Dakkar stared, amazed, as a whole world flew by. Dolphins raced alongside, their bodies undulating as they struggled to keep pace with the *Makara*. Dakkar laughed aloud.

A terrible thought broke through his exhilaration, and he slammed the boat to a halt and surfaced. Only the small section of the *Makara* broke the surface; the vast bulk remained below.

In the distance, on the cliff, the castle burned.

Mrs Evans was dead, murdered by the hideous man in the hall. Oginski had been taken. A tight band of guilt closed round Dakkar's chest. Tears scalded his cheeks as image after image of the deadly encounter in the castle forced its way into his mind.

Why did this happen? What can I do? The questions

rolled over and over in Dakkar's mind, like the waves that lapped against the sides of the *Makara*.

Dakkar knew. 'Blizzard,' he said, staring at his reflection in the porthole. His dark hair was matted with sweat and tears stained his cheeks, but his eyes blazed with fury. 'Blizzard is to blame. Whoever that man was in the hall, he worked for Blizzard, I'm certain. Blizzard said he would return.'

A cold numbness enveloped Dakkar. He steered for the castle and waited just beneath the surface.

The afternoon passed slowly. Oginski had told him to flee to his father, but first he would make Blizzard pay.

Blizzard had said that his ship was moored in Fullacombe Harbour. By Dakkar's reckoning, it wouldn't have passed the castle yet. The day was dying rapidly – the fire on the cliffs burned more brightly, reflecting the fire in Dakkar's heart.

Soon the darkness out to sea seemed so complete, so full, absorbing everything. In the large lower cabin, Dakkar found a hatch up to the front of the *Makara*. He popped his head out and squinted into the blackness, listening hard above the roar of the waves and the slap of water against the side of the boat.

A feeble bell rang the hour. Dakkar caught his breath. *A ship's bell!* In the darkness a deeper shadow drifted by, her sails ghostly white in the moonlight. With her rows of cannon along her side, she was unmistakably a warship. *It has to be Blizzard's ship!*

Dakkar climbed back into the *Makara* and pushed the power lever to *Full Ahead*. 'Now I'll send Blizzard and all his men to their deaths, and serve them right!'

CHAPTER SIX
COLLISION COURSE

Dakkar gritted his teeth and set the *Makara* on a collision course with the warship. In his mind's eye, he saw the submersible ramming into its side, the sharp metal-encased nose of the *Makara* splintering the planks. Men falling into the sea. Rigging collapsing to the deck. Fires raging in the hold.

He pushed at the lever. Blizzard would pay.

A memory of Oginski sprang into his mind, from soon after his arrival at the castle. He and his mentor were sitting on a rough outcrop of rock high up on the cliffs, their feet dangling over the waves that battered at the rocks way below. Dakkar felt small but anger blazed in the pit of his stomach.

'You ran away again!' Oginski said, his voice low. 'That's twice in two weeks.'

'But you teach me nothing,' Dakkar snapped. 'I do nothing but swim in this freezing sea all the time. I hate swimming. I hate the sea! What use is that to me?'

'Why did your father send you to me?' Oginski asked.

'To learn how to drive out those who would interfere with our country,' Dakkar said. 'To take revenge on those who try to crush our people!'

'He who takes revenge often sacrifices himself,' Oginski murmured. 'Does a great leader trade blow for blow? Or does he become wiser, more powerful than his enemies?'

'What's that supposed to mean?' Dakkar snarled, but Oginski's face remained stern.

'Men can become so consumed by revenge that they become monsters,' Oginski whispered, holding Dakkar's gaze.

The whine of the engine brought Dakkar back from his memories. The *Makara* ploughed the surface, sending fountains of spray hammering against the portholes. Dakkar could see the planks of the ship, the gun ports. He could see men moving around on the decks and in the rigging. In a few seconds it would all be over.

'Are you a monster?' Oginski's voice echoed in his mind.

Alarm bells rang out on the ship.

Dakkar slammed the lever to *Stop* and whisked the ballast wheel clockwise. Slowly the *Makara* sank beneath the waves.

He couldn't sink Blizzard's ship.

Besides, Oginski is on board, Dakkar thought. *If I sink the ship he might drown.*

Dakkar stared out of the porthole as, slowly, the black shadow of the ship's hull passed over his head and the *Makara* drifted down to the depths.

'I'll have to be more devious,' he muttered to himself.

He could follow them. Watch the guard and the routines of the ship. Choose his moment and slip in to rescue Oginski.

Dakkar's stomach gave a loud grumble and he suddenly felt hungry. He realised that he hadn't eaten since yesterday. He gave a groan. Here he was in a strange vessel, expecting to follow a ship some three thousand miles across the sea. He would need food.

It occurred to Dakkar that if he surfaced near the ship during the day, Blizzard's crew would easily spot him. Following the ship wasn't going to be easy. He'd have to sleep of course, but the ship would sail on through the night. He rubbed his tired eyes at the thought of staying awake and peered up at the black bulk of the ship above him. *If I can follow beneath the ship, they may not notice me*, he thought. *Then perhaps I can fall back out of sight in the morning and go up top for air.*

He looked down at himself. He was still wearing his grubby, stained nightshirt. Nothing else. *How can I do anything in this?*

Dakkar stopped the *Makara* and clambered down into the lower cabin, searching for anything that might prove useful. A ship's trunk contained some jars of pickled herring, some hard biscuits, a length of fishing line and hooks, netting, and various brass rings and bolts. A compass sat amid the closely packed equipment. At the bottom, a pair of trousers and a flannel shirt lay neatly folded. Holding them up, Dakkar could see they were much too big but he shrugged and pulled them on anyway, tying a length of rope round his waist for a belt.

Oginski really did think of everything. He grinned, opened a jar of herrings and bit into the vinegary fish. His eyes watered and the vinegar burned his throat but it tasted so good. Behind the passenger seat, Dakkar took a skin of water from the wall. The water was a little brackish and had obviously been there for some time. *Better than dying of thirst*, Dakkar thought, sipping carefully.

For a while, Dakkar felt refreshed by the food. He restarted the *Makara* and was amazed at how quickly he caught up with Blizzard's ship. He followed beneath the ship, keeping an eye on its huge silhouette against the moonlit surface of the sea and mulling over the events of the day. Dakkar shuddered at the memory of the strange fish-men in the cavern, their lifeless eyes and scaly skin. *Why does Blizzard have such strange henchmen?*

Dakkar changed his line of thought. He didn't want to think of the fish-men. Thoughts of them swimming alongside the *Makara*, slamming their webbed fingers against the portholes, made him peer nervously out into the gloom of the sea.

So what is Blizzard's plan? Does he think Oginski will change his mind just because he kidnapped him?

Blizzard's ship ploughed on through the waves and Dakkar steered the *Makara* underneath. The whine of the engine and the gentle rocking of the craft began to soothe Dakkar's tormented mind. His eyes drooped and his head nodded, bringing him back to startled wakefulness. *Mustn't fall asleep*, he told himself. But gradually his head sank to his chest and the exhaustion of the day overtook him.

Dakkar woke with a start. Something bumped and banged about his head but he couldn't quite work out where he was. Then, with a lurch, he realised.

'No, no, no, no,' he hissed through gritted teeth, peering out of the porthole.

Daylight shone through the sea's surface. Dakkar marvelled that he'd stayed with Blizzard's ship even in his sleep – but the *Makara* had risen to the level of the ship's hull. A grinding sound vibrated through the *Makara* as it bounced along the keel.

With a curse, Dakkar twisted the wheel, sending the craft back down. He pulled the drive lever to *Stop* and watched as the warship pulled away. Dakkar's head thumped and the air tasted thick and stale. *I could've suffocated*, he thought. But even more urgent matters pressed as Dakkar realised his bladder was fit to burst.

He let the ship go ahead of him and then surfaced. Opening the hatch at the front of the craft, Dakkar popped his head out and then climbed on to the deck. He'd been on sailing ships before and had rowed in the sea but he'd never felt as small and insignificant as he did now. The ocean stretched out, grey and rolling, all around him. In the distance, Dakkar could see the top of the ship's mast. The *Makara* rose and fell on the great blue-and-white hills that rolled across the surface of the sea. She pitched and tossed dangerously, threatening to tip Dakkar into the water, especially when he tried relieving himself over the side. He half crouched, half stood, swaying and correcting his balance as he went. Dakkar took a few deep breaths, enjoying the chill salt breeze on his face, then slipped down below.

As he walked through the lower cabin, he noticed the cupboard by the table and pulled the door open. Rolled-up charts were piled on top of each other but beneath them one lay flat. Dakkar dragged it out. It was another plan like the one he'd seen in the castle cellar, but this plan showed how the two boats fitted together. He noticed labels detailing different features of the *Makara*: a snorkel in the roof that poked above sea level and fed air into the cabin, an auger that could drill into the hulls of enemy ships. But not all of the handwriting was Oginski's. Another hand had added labels. Dakkar shifted the plans on to the table and a sheaf of letters fell to the floor. He picked one up. Dakkar caught a glimpse of a name, written in fine spidery writing: *Your Servant, Robert Fulton*.

Dakkar opened the letter and smoothed it out. The date stood out at the top, *20th July 1813*.

Has Oginski been writing to Fulton? Dakkar thought, frowning. He read on:

My Dearest Oginski,

I feel you may be nearer the prize than I. Your description of the miniature pump system to make more room for the ballast is genius and is sure to solve the problem . . .

Dakkar leafed through the pile of papers. There were documents, more plans and diagrams with scribbled notes in Fulton's handwriting. As he read, Dakkar saw how the *Makara* had grown and developed. Oginski would pose a problem to Fulton, or Fulton would anticipate a difficulty, and they would discuss it at length in their correspondence.

'Fulton was helping Oginski to build the *Makara*!' Dakkar whispered.

If Blizzard finds these, Oginski would be hanged as a traitor or a spy, he thought, the papers shaking in his hand.

Dakkar stared down at the letters. He didn't have time to read all of them now – Blizzard's ship had disappeared over the horizon and, although Oginski had taught him about plotting a course and navigating with a map, compass and stars, Dakkar felt more confident keeping Blizzard in sight. But the plans gave Dakkar a greater idea of what the *Makara* was capable of.

He stowed the papers away securely and clambered up into his seat. Pushing the lever to full power, he grinned, waiting for the now familiar whirr and click of the engine. Nothing happened. With a hiss, Dakkar jumped back down to the crank handle in the lower cabin – it needed winding up.

Dakkar turned the handle, quickly and easily at first. His shoulders began to burn as he spun the crank round. He paused, panting. After what seemed like an age, the crank became harder to turn. Dakkar's arms felt like putty as he turned and turned. With a final gasp, he pushed the handle one last time and stumbled back, sweat trickling down his back.

I might be halfway to New York by now! he thought, dragging himself up into the captain's seat. He slammed the lever and the *Makara* lurched forward.

Spray rattled at the window as the *Makara* sliced through the waves. Dakkar fumbled above his head for the snorkel handle he'd seen on the plan. A few turns of a wheel found him basking in a flow of cool sea air that blew in from the tube overhead.

But Dakkar felt the heaviness of dread in his stomach. The horizon looked flat and empty. Where had the ship gone? A black speck became a mast which then became . . .

'Two masts?' Dakkar said aloud, his jaw dropping.

Tiny wisps of smoke billowed up from each ship. Splashes of white foam plumed into the air around both of them where the cannonballs hit the water. The ships grew in size and Dakkar could see tongues of flame spitting from the gun ports, wreaths of black smoke choking the decks. The Union Jack fluttered from the stern of Blizzard's ship. A black flag hung from the other.

'Pirates!' Dakkar gasped. 'And if Blizzard's ship goes down Oginski goes down with it!'

CHAPTER SEVEN
DISASTER

The sounds of battle grew louder as the *Makara* surged towards the ships. Dakkar flinched at the sound of cannon fire and even more at the sound of shot punching the water. *If one of those cannonballs hits the* Makara, *I'm doomed!*

To make matters worse, one of the pirate ship's masts had been blown apart, leaving rigging and loose spars of wood fouling the water. And, just below the surface, with blood seeping from their wounds, the dead floated, their clothes billowing in the currents created by the ships. Dakkar shuddered.

He peered up at the pirate ship's hull. He thought of what he might have done in his rage when he first encountered Blizzard's ship. A head-on impact with the ship's thick planks would have sunk her, but he had no doubt that the *Makara* would have been destroyed too. No, he had to be cunning.

Steering the *Makara* under Blizzard's vessel, Dakkar described a wide circle and headed back for the pirate ship. At the stern, he could see the rudder and the chains that pulled it left and right. It was a solid piece of wood but not as thick as the hull itself. *That's her weak point.* His mind was made up.

The side of the pirate ship loomed over Dakkar, getting closer by the second. Dakkar's heart thumped against his ribs; he held his breath. He could see the nails hammered into the planks, barnacles clinging to the side, and then the *Makara* shuddered as her metal beak tore into the rudder. Dakkar flew off his seat from the impact and fell down into the lower cabin. The sound of rending metal and wood deafened him. The *Makara* slowed, something thudding against her, then she shot clear.

Dakkar turned the *Makara* round just in time to see the fragmented rudder sinking into the darkness below him. He shook his fist and grinned. It was better than he'd hoped. Part of the hull had been ripped out with the rudder. The pirate ship listed as she took on water through the hole. Suddenly, the whole stern of the ship slipped below the surface. Glass windows shattered as furniture slid out. Cannon smashed through gun ports and plummeted to the invisible seabed.

More of the starboard side of the ship sank below the surface. Nets and coils of rope, barrels and sacks spilt into the water. Dakkar stared at the wreckage.

The cabin suddenly darkened and he realised how close he had come to the foundering ship. A thick shadow fell across his portholes and Dakkar's ears popped with the roaring as, seemingly from nowhere, a huge piece of mast smashed down on to the *Makara*, punching its way into the small cabin where Dakkar sat.

Water filled the cabin and knocked Dakkar out of his seat. He gasped at the cold water as it pummelled him down through the hole into the lower cabin. He slapped at the sides of the hatch but the wall of water thumped him in the stomach, sending him to the floor. Water forced its way up his nose, into his mouth, making him gag.

The sea swirled around the lower cabin, causing a confusion of furniture, papers and boxes. Pain lanced through Dakkar's temple as something struck him. He tried to stand but was plunged into the water.

Gasping for breath, Dakkar threw himself towards the front of the cabin and fumbled with the forward hatch. Bubbles rushed by the large portholes as the *Makara* sank. The hatch unlocked and Dakkar lunged forward, wriggling and kicking his way out.

Above him the mottling of light on the sea surface seemed an eternity away. A bizarre rain of chains, rivets, boxes and barrels surrounded him, making him dodge back and forth as he struggled for the surface.

Dakkar's lungs ached with the effort. He'd barely had the chance to take a breath before kicking his way up and now he was paying for it. His head spun and his arms felt like sponge. A pulley block hurtled towards him, flailing rope in its wake like some deadly jellyfish. Dakkar twisted his body to one side, kicking frantically as the rope from the pulley snapped at his feet and ankles.

Every muscle in Dakkar's body burned with agony as he kicked his feet and heaved himself upward through the boiling water. His head felt as if it would burst. Small bubbles of air began to pop from his lips. He could taste the salt water in his mouth. The surface hovered somewhere out of reach above his head. He screamed silently as he pummelled the sea with cupped hands.

Suddenly the cold air hit him as his head broke the water. Dakkar's throat stung as he gulped at the fresh air. The world was a confusion of shouting and smoke. Flotsam littered the surface as Dakkar floundered, splashing his arms about to stay afloat. He grabbed at a plank that drifted past, dragged himself over it and lay panting.

The *Makara* was gone.

The smoke swirled around him, making shadowy ghosts of the wreckage that floated with him. He coughed and choked, sea water burning his throat as he spewed it up. Other voices cried out now. Desperate, pleading voices. Every now and then one would weaken and fall silent. The cold water began to gnaw at Dakkar's core, making his teeth chatter and loosening his grip on the plank. He kicked his legs as best he could but the sea had numbed them. His vision began to whiten, light filling his sight, blotting out the details until he couldn't see. He felt the grain of the wood slide from out of his grasp. The sting of water on his face brought him to and he splashed feebly.

'There's one here!' a voice cried. 'A boy. We can't leave him.'

Dakkar felt strong hands grip under his arms and he became weightless. The water vanished and instead he felt the press of planks at the bottom of a rowing boat.

'Take him and these others to Blizzard,' said a gruff voice. 'Find out what they know. The rest of you, save anything valuable that's floating.'

The voices faded and darkness finally filled Dakkar's vision as exhaustion took him.

The market square buzzed with life. Bordering the square, stalls were piled high with spices and fruit. The sweet smell of spiced chicken roasting on hot coals taunted Dakkar's nostrils as he looked down at the throng from his balcony. Traders in colourful robes jostled with travel-weary merchants. Women with heavy baskets chided ragged children who chased in and out between the grumbling adults. In the centre of the square stood a wooden platform.

'Look at them, my son,' his father said, placing a hand on Dakkar's shoulder. 'They are the herd. Farmers, shepherds, cooks and merchants. They need a leader. They need someone to fear.'

'Yes, Father,' Dakkar said, puzzled, as the rajah raised a hand.

The crowd parted and three royal guards dragged a struggling man through the dust to the platform. Two guards slammed the ragged man to his knees on the platform while the other one read a proclamation.

'He spied on me for the English,' Dakkar's father sneered. 'For the British East India Company.'

'But doesn't the Peshwa tell us that they are our friends?' Dakkar wondered aloud.

His father's face darkened. 'The Peshwa is a fool!' he spat. 'He is meant to govern us all but he is a mere puppet, controlled by the company.'

Dakkar stared at the hatred on his father's face. Then a scream snapped his head back to the square. Blood pooled on the platform and the guard tossed something into the crowd. Dakkar turned away.

'Watch, my son,' his father whispered, close to his ear. 'That is how a true leader deals with enemies.'

Freezing water smacked Dakkar in the face, stopping his breath and making him sit upright. His hands gripped dirty straw strewn on a damp wooden floor. The smell of tar and stale bodies filled his nostrils and drove the roast-chicken scent of his dreams far away.

In the semi-light, Dakkar saw rough walls, a small door with a barred window. Two seamen blocked the door. One tall and bony, with protruding cheekbones and ears like trophy handles. The other filled more of the doorway, with his round belly and broad shoulders. His goatee beard made him seem as though he had a constant smirk on his face.

'The boy, Mr Slater,' said the fat man. 'He wants the boy.'

'Aye, Mr Finch,' said the bony Mr Slater, with a long sad smile. 'None of you others now. Stand back!'

Dakkar turned round and saw a gaggle of eight evil-looking men. He suppressed a whimper as he took in eyepatches and hooks, scars and sneers.

The nearest pirate leered at Dakkar with one good eye, his grin displaying crooked brown teeth. 'Put a good word in fer us, eh, lad?' he cackled, and poked Dakkar in the shoulder. The other pirates all joined in, shoving and laughing at him.

Finch grabbed Dakkar's shoulder with pudgy hands and dragged him out of the room. Slater slammed the door shut and turned the key in the lock.

'You're in with a bad lot there, lad,' Slater muttered, shaking his head.

Dakkar stumbled through the darkened lower decks of the ship. Men scurried around, hammering wood, heaving broken barrels and sweeping the floor. They only paused to glare at him. *Where is Oginski? He must be on the ship somewhere, surely?*

Blizzard's ship looked to be in bad shape. Blood stained the steps to the upper deck and Dakkar grimaced as he tried to step over it.

'That was spilt by a good friend of mine,' Finch growled. 'I 'ope they hang you from the highest yardarm, me laddo.'

The daylight dazzled Dakkar as he staggered up on deck. The crew were hurrying up and down rigging, and the sound of shouting, hammering and sawing rang across the ship.

'We didn't fare too badly,' a voice called out from above him. Dakkar turned and recognised the scar-faced commander standing on the quarterdeck at the stern of the ship. Blizzard leaned on the rails and stared down at Dakkar. 'We'll soon be back to full sail and on our mission again. So, boy, welcome aboard the *Palaemon*.'

'Where's Oginski?' Dakkar hissed.

'Oginski?' Blizzard frowned, peering closer at Dakkar. Then his eyes widened. 'Good Lord! It's you, Oginski's prince! But how is that possible? And why are you consorting with pirates?'

'You broke into our castle,' Dakkar said angrily. 'You killed Mrs Evans and took Oginski away.'

'I took him away?' Blizzard repeated, and he started to laugh. 'You think I'm holding Oginski on this ship?'

'Your monsters kidnapped him,' Dakkar said through clenched teeth.

Blizzard's mirth evaporated. His face hardened. 'I did intend to send some men to search the premises – I suspect Oginski might be withholding some secrets from us – but I didn't have him taken.'

'You're lying!' Dakkar snarled, taking a step forward.

Slater and Finch reached for him. Dakkar ducked under their grasp. He rushed at the commander but found himself with the point of Blizzard's sword at his throat.

Blizzard fixed Dakkar with an icy glare. 'If you were a grown man,' he said in a low voice, 'I'd kill you for calling me a liar. As it is, I'll put your poor manners down to a bad upbringing and youthful folly. Keep a civil tongue in your head or I'll cut it out.'

Dakkar stood stock-still. 'I don't understand,' he said. 'I was certain Oginski was on this ship. You said you were coming back for him!'

'That was a bit of a bluff, if I'm honest,' Blizzard said, sheathing his sword. 'And Oginski would have known that.'

Dakkar shook his head, still unwilling to believe the truth. He felt hollow and empty. Chasing after Blizzard had been for nothing and now he was trapped on this ship miles from home, with the Makara lying smashed at the bottom of the ocean. Tears stung his eyes and he stared down at the deck, fighting them back.

'But if Oginski isn't here, who *has* taken him?' he murmured.

'That,' Blizzard said, 'is a good question. But a better one is why shouldn't I have you hanged like a common pirate? Take hold of him – now!'

Slater advanced on Dakkar, while Finch coiled a rope.

CHAPTER EIGHT
NO ANSWERS

Finch and Slater grabbed Dakkar and pinned his arms to his sides with the rope.

'I should warn you that my men are in no mood to trifle,' Blizzard said. 'They lost some good friends today and are thirsty for revenge.'

'Aye,' Slater snarled. 'Let's string him up, sir, and those other dogs in the hold!'

'Steady, Slater,' Blizzard said, raising a calming hand. 'Now, *your highness*, suppose you tell me how it's possible for me to see you but a couple of days ago at your home in England and then meet you again here on a pirate vessel that has doubtless come from the other side of the ocean?'

'I flew,' Dakkar sneered, which earned him a chubby backhand over the head from Finch.

'I'm not an idiot, Prince Dakkar,' Blizzard said. 'Oh yes, I know precisely who you are. I keep my ear to the ground, so to speak. My spies are everywhere.'

Dakkar pursed his lips and ignored Blizzard's game.

'Let's have a think,' Blizzard said, pacing the deck. 'You live in a castle where the locals tell stories of strange sea monsters, of peculiar noises in the night. And Oginski is a brilliant inventor – did you know he tried to sell the navy plans for a manned balloon before the Montgolfier brothers flew? His was far better but my short-sighted superiors couldn't think of a use for it.'

'I was being sarcastic when I said I flew,' Dakkar sneered.

'You can laugh but I'd almost believe you. Oginski is a genius,' Blizzard replied. 'And then, just as we leave Britain, we see a strange sight approaching us. My lookout said we were nearly rammed by some kind of whale.'

'I wish it had rammed you,' Dakkar muttered.

'Oginski was working with Fulton on an underwater boat, wasn't he?' Blizzard said suddenly. 'You took it thinking Oginski was on board my ship.'

'No,' Dakkar said, his cheeks reddening.

'Fulton developed a fully functional submersible over ten years ago,' Blizzard said. 'He tried to sell the design to the French and to us, but again people were short-sighted. I think he continued working on it, refining it, with Oginski's help.'

'I don't know anything about this!' Dakkar yelled, tears streaming down his face. 'Someone has taken Oginski. I just want to find him!'

'So you had nothing to do with the sudden and mysterious destruction of the pirate ship's rudder?' Blizzard said in a low voice. 'Take him back down below.'

Dakkar remained silent as Slater and Finch led him back to the hold and the pirates. They opened the door and threw him in.

The pirates all stared at him as he stumbled through the door. He squatted on the ground, his head bowed. *If they knew I'd sunk their ship, they'd kill me!* he thought.

'So he threw you back, did he?' the one-eyed pirate cackled. His long beak-like nose made Dakkar think of an old crow. 'You were pulled out of the water, weren't you?'

'What of it?' Dakkar said, shrugging and eyeing the pirate.

'So where'd you come from then? Stowaway? Fall from the sky?' His one good eye glittered in the gloom.

'Stowaway,' Dakkar muttered. 'I fell in when they lowered the lifeboats.'

'Really?' The pirate grinned. Dakkar shuddered. 'When you was out for the count before, you was doin' a lot o' talkin' an' mutterin' in your sleep, like.'

'I have bad dreams.' Dakkar blushed.

'I'll bet you do, if they involve Oginski,' the pirate said, and sniggered as Dakkar's head snapped up.

'What d'you mean?' Dakkar asked, glaring at the man.

'That's a cursed name,' said a pirate close by. His golden earrings sparkled against his ebony skin. 'Oginski is a name to fear.'

'He don't know the story,' One-eye said. 'Albie, you tell it well.'

An old man, with a straggly, grey beard and a scar across his neck, shuffled forward and took a deep breath.

'Once, a long time ago – not in your lifetime, but in mine – there lived a count and a countess, and they were very happy. God had blessed them with a castle, rich vineyards and a land of such beauty that it could barely be imagined.

'But their crowning glory, their true blessing, was their seven sons. Each was handsome, each was clever and each had a particular skill. One was a great soldier, another could coax animals from the trees, while another built inventions that would baffle dukes and ladies across the land with their ingenuity and craft. These boys were always competing with each other to see who could ride the fastest, jump the highest, drink the most, sing the loudest. They were so full of life.

'Sad to say, nothing lasts for ever, be it good or bad, and such was the case for the count and countess. All seven sons fell in love. With the same woman. Her name was Celina, a wondrous beauty; her hair was like spun gold and her lips like roses. When she sang, it put the nightingale to shame.

'As beauteous as Celina was, she could never marry one of the count's sons. Her father was a simple wood-cutter, a peasant. But the boys would bring her gifts every day, sing her songs every day, write poems in honour of her great beauty every day. She didn't know what to do.

' "Set each boy a task," her father said. "Make them travel.

The experience will do them good and when they have seen more of the world they will no longer think of you."

'Celina wasn't so sure about this – she quite liked the attentions of the handsome young men – but if the count found out that his sons were courting a commoner he would be furious, and who knew what he would do?

'So Celina sent them abroad, and such adventures they had and such sights they saw. But they never forgot her. Each carried a miniature portrait of her in his breast pocket, next to his heart, and after twelve long months the boys returned.

'To horror.

'Their castle lay in ruins, the vineyards burned to the scorched earth, their mother and father cruelly slain. And of Celina there was no trace.

'For, while they had been travelling, the tsar's troops had swept across the land in the name of Holy Russia. Any who stood in their path felt the edge of their sword, the rough hemp rope or the heat of flame.

'Grief does strange things to a man, and as the seven brothers stood there they made a vow to avenge their father, their mother and the lovely Celina.

'They became bitter, hard and as cold as steel. As the years flew by, they drowned their grief in an orgy of bloodshed and violence. People learned to fear the name of the Brothers Oginski.'

For a moment, silence hung over the dingy hold as each listener took from the story what they could.

'A fairytale,' Dakkar said, snorting. 'The Oginski I know is a man of science, and a gentleman.'

'Who knows what past wickedness men hide,' One-eye sniggered. 'At least we're honest rogues.' He leaned back against the wall of the hold. 'What you see is what you get.'

The days rolled into weeks and the pirates were set to work on the *Palaemon* under the watchful eye of Blizzard's marines. Dakkar found himself scrubbing decks and helping Finch prepare food in the galley.

Every day left Dakkar with a gnawing anxiety. Questions built up in his mind. *Who were the strange men at the castle that day? What did they want with Oginski?* Every mile they sailed was taking him further away from any chance of rescuing Oginski. Blizzard questioned him further but Dakkar kept silent and refused to answer.

'So what did you call this undersea ship that Oginski and Fulton created?' Blizzard asked matter-of-factly, as if he were asking Dakkar what he'd had for dinner.

'I don't know what you're talking about, sir,' Dakkar said, and continued with his polishing work. 'It sounds a bit fanciful, if you'll pardon me for saying.'

'Fanciful,' Blizzard mused. 'Yes, I suppose it does, but then everything about you is a bit far-fetched, Prince Dakkar. Did you know, for instance, that your father has offered a reward for your recovery?'

Dakkar stiffened and he looked up at Blizzard. 'My father?' he said. 'He must have heard about what happened at the castle.'

'No,' Blizzard replied, turning to walk away. 'This reward was offered three or four years ago.'

'What?' Dakkar said, leaping to his feet, but Blizzard sauntered away and Finch glared at Dakkar until he sat down to his polishing again.

Night-times on the HMS *Palaemon* were a torment of snoring pirates, the uncomfortable hold floor and whirling thoughts. Dakkar dismissed the pirate's story as just that. *There's bound to be more than one Oginski in the world.* But now a new question pressed in on Dakkar: *why did Father offer a reward?*

For a few days, the weather turned against them. Dakkar lay prostrate in the hold as the *Palaemon* rose and fell, making his stomach heave. He couldn't move or eat. When he did go outside, the sea lashed the deck and the horizon pitched up and down. Dakkar imagined being trapped in the *Makara* on the mountainous waves that surrounded them and shuddered. All the time he wondered how he would get off the ship and find Oginski.

'Fulton's the key,' Blizzard said one day, making Dakkar jump as he scrubbed at the decking with a stiff brush. 'If you want to find Oginski, I mean.'

The weather had calmed and, although the sky hung sullen and grey, the winds had dropped.

'With respect, sir,' Dakkar said, looking at his feet, 'Oginski barely knew Mr Fulton.'

'Whatever you say,' Blizzard sighed, clamping his hands behind his back. 'Once we've destroyed this steam battery of Fulton's, we'll be returning to England and then it's the gallows for you, boy.'

'You won't be claiming the reward my father is said to have offered?' Dakkar asked, looking up at Blizzard.

The commander laughed. 'If a court finds you guilty of piracy – and you *were* caught in the company of pirates – then, prince or no, you will hang. I have no interest in money or wealth. I live only to serve my country.'

And you're well paid for it into the bargain, Dakkar thought, eyeing Blizzard's fine coat and breeches.

'And why exactly did my father offer such a reward?' Dakkar said, unable to keep the contempt from leeching into his voice.

'Why, because you vanished, young man,' Blizzard said with a short laugh. 'Presumed kidnapped. But no ransom was demanded – some thought you dead.'

A scream cut Dakkar's next question short. He turned and stared in horror at the thing that was crawling on to the ship.

CHAPTER NINE
THE CREATURE FROM THE DEPTHS

A huge red tentacle gripped a sailor and whisked him from the deck. Dakkar caught the look of horror in his staring eyes as he vanished, dragged over the side and into the sea. Water rained down on the deck as more tentacles squirmed their way across the deck or through the rigging. Men's shouts of anger or terror mingled with the odd gunshot.

Dakkar hurried over to the railings and saw a giant eye staring up from the sea, the huge bulk of the body tapering off into the depths.

'A giant squid,' he gasped. 'I saw one off the coast the day before –'

'Quickly, Dakkar – down below,' Blizzard yelled. He took a step forward but a tentacle reached up over the side and curled round his leg.

Blizzard gave a howl as the fabric of his breeches tore under its grip. Dakkar could see the serrated suckers on the tentacle drawing blood.

Snatching up an axe, Dakkar leapt forward and hacked into the rubbery flesh of the squid. The creature quivered but continued to drag Blizzard along the deck to the side of the ship. Dakkar hacked and hacked again. Another tentacle swooped down, swatting at Dakkar. He dodged to one side, feeling the thick arm swish just above his head. With a yell, he brought the axe down on the creature's twitching limb. The axe struck through flesh and bit into the hard deck, numbing Dakkar's arm with the impact. Blizzard collapsed, gripping his injured leg as the severed tentacle writhed and twisted close by.

More tentacles squirmed towards Dakkar, tipping a rowing boat over and spilling its contents on to the deck. Dakkar snatched up a long boat hook that rolled to his feet and he stabbed it at the flailing arms.

Finch swirled past, bellowing obscenities from the end of a snaking squid arm. Dakkar hurled the boat hook and smiled with grim satisfaction as it pierced the arm. Finch gave a strangled cry and plummeted on to the deck with a thud.

The crew had rallied now and Blizzard's marines in their red coats hurried forward, firing musket shot after musket shot until the squid blew a fountain of black ink into the air and slid back into the water.

Dakkar scurried across the slimy deck to where Blizzard lay. His leg looked torn and bloodied but he managed a grin at Dakkar.

'Thank you,' he panted. 'I think you just saved my life.'

For some time, the crew stumbled around in mute wonder, uncertain of what they had just experienced. They took Blizzard to his cabin and went through the motions of clearing up and counting the dead. The shocked silence that followed the attack hung over them like a storm cloud.

'It's a curse,' Slater whispered, pointing a bony finger at Dakkar. 'It's that boy. He's brought bad luck on us!'

The sailors gathered around him, murmuring their disquiet. Dakkar's heart pounded. He looked from one angry face to the next.

'He just appeared from the sea,' one of the pirates called from the back of the crowd. 'He wasn't with us.'

'Funny how *he* managed to fight the beast off,' Slater hissed. 'But it was throwin' the rest of us around the ship like a shark playin' with seal pups!'

'Leave him be, Slater,' Finch said, stepping forward. 'The boy saved my life. I'd have been squid fodder if it weren't for him.'

'No, I reckon he's brought bad luck on us all,' Slater snarled, bringing his face close to Finch's. 'Throw him overboard, I say!'

'You'll have to get past me first!' Finch growled back. 'This boy is a hero – you should be thankin' him!'

Finch squared his shoulders and stared into Slater's eyes. Dakkar watched the two men glaring at each other. Finch was a big man but Slater looked wiry and fast.

A gunshot broke the tension and made everyone turn. Blizzard leaned against the door to his cabin, a pistol in his hand. A white bandage swathed his leg and he looked pale and feverish.

'The boy is under my protection,' he gasped. 'Slater, unless you want flogging, I suggest you refrain from stirring up trouble.'

'But, sir, I was only suggestin' –' Slater began.

'One more word out of you, man, and I'll have you clapped in irons,' Blizzard snapped, wincing a little. 'Now, everyone back to their duties. This ship doesn't sail herself. Finch, sort a hammock out for Dakkar down below – he's no longer a prisoner.'

'Aye, sir,' Finch said, grinning and winking at Dakkar. He leaned down and whispered, 'Don't worry, lad. I'll stay close by you.'

The following morning, Dakkar found Blizzard limping along the quarterdeck. He had a stick and, although he looked pale, he seemed in better spirits.

'Dakkar,' he said, patting him on the shoulder, 'you fought that beast off valiantly yesterday.'

'I didn't feel very valiant,' Dakkar said, blushing. 'My father taught me how to fight with a lance, though I usually practised on horseback. Where did the giant squid come from? And why did it attack?'

'Who knows?' Blizzard shrugged. 'It's very strange to encounter such a beast this far north.'

'You've seen them before?' Dakkar asked, his eyes widening.

'Yes, but never that big,' Blizzard said, nodding. He grew

more serious. 'And it *is* strange that it just popped out of the ocean and attacked us. Of course if I knew half of what was going on, maybe I could make some sense of it.' He gave Dakkar a wry look and Dakkar glanced away to the horizon.

'I have to find Oginski,' Dakkar murmured.

'We're nearing our destination,' Blizzard said, shifting his position a little and suppressing a wince. 'I know you maintain that Oginski and Fulton aren't in contact, but if they were then I'd say that he might be worth a visit. I know roughly where Fulton's home is. I could take a slight detour and my men could put you ashore. You'd be on your own though, and the Americans don't take kindly to spies.'

'You'd do that for me?' Dakkar said, wondering at Blizzard's sudden change of heart.

'I owe you my life, Dakkar,' Blizzard said, looking solemn. 'I'm a man of honour and I see my debts paid.'

'Then you could tell me more about this alleged reward that my father offered,' Dakkar said, suddenly feeling bold.

'All I know is what I told you yesterday,' Blizzard said, shrugging. 'Four years ago, you went missing. Your father offered a reward.'

'But Father sent me to Oginski,' Dakkar insisted. 'He was to be my mentor.'

'It does seem strange,' Blizzard said, raising his eyebrows. 'A father offers a reward for his missing son, when all along he knows he's safe. What did your father say in his letters?'

'Letters?' Dakkar repeated. 'I didn't get any. He wanted my location to be a secret from his enemies and so made no contact.'

'I found you,' Blizzard said, a slight smile twisting the unscarred half of his face. 'There's not much gossip that doesn't reach my ears and the fisherfolk of the village were very chatty. Someone else did too, by the sound of it. Could it have been your father?'

'My own father who kidnapped Oginski and murdered Mrs Evans?' Dakkar spluttered. 'Why would he do that when he could just tell Oginski to send me home?'

Blizzard gave another lopsided smile. He looked sad. 'Maybe he couldn't. Oginski is a law unto himself – you know that. What if your father couldn't get you back?'

'Oginski would never do that,' Dakkar said, horrified. 'He'd never hold me against my will. Maybe my father put out the reward to confuse his enemies!'

Blizzard nodded his head slowly, but whether he was agreeing Dakkar couldn't tell.

Dakkar stamped down the steps from the quarter-deck. *I should be pleased*, he thought. *If I can find Fulton, then maybe I'll have a clue as to who took Oginski.* But the conversation about the reward nagged at him.

The next few days saw Dakkar on light duties – Finch and Blizzard made sure of that. Dakkar kept out of the way of Slater, who glowered at him whenever they crossed paths.

Finally, one evening, the lookout shouted and Dakkar ran forward to see a distant strip of grey on the horizon.

'Americay!' Finch laughed. 'We'll have to be careful, mind – there'll be patrols back and forth, and if anyone spots us from shore they'll sound the alarm.'

Dakkar stared at the indistinct mass in the distance. His stomach twisted and he felt like telling Blizzard that he'd changed his mind. What if Fulton didn't know anything? What if he were caught and hanged as a spy?

'You don't have to go, y'know,' Finch said, giving Dakkar a sidelong glance. 'I don't reckon Blizzard would be for seein' yer hang when we get back to England.'

'No,' Dakkar muttered, shaking his head. 'If there's a chance of finding Oginski, then I must take it.'

'Ship to starboard!' cried the lookout, sending Finch and Dakkar scurrying over to the other side of the ship.

'Look lively, men!' Blizzard bellowed from the quarter-deck. He limped over to starboard and pulled open his telescope.

Sailors ran to and fro. Some hurried to the cannon that lined the deck; others scrambled down below.

'Is she American?' Dakkar asked, clambering up the steps to Blizzard.

'Hard to tell, lad,' Blizzard murmured. 'I can't make out her colours yet but we can't be too careful. We must get ready for a fight.'

'I'll need a weapon then,' Dakkar said, narrowing his eyes at the horizon.

'Of course – I didn't expect you to be cowering in the hold, Prince!' Blizzard laughed, and patted Dakkar on the back. 'Go with Finch and choose your weapons.'

'Come with me, lad,' Finch said, grinning.

Dakkar followed Finch down to the main deck, where marines were giving out swords, pistols and powder.

'Arm the pirates too,' Blizzard called over the crowd. 'They'll fight for their lives as well as any.'

Soon, Dakkar stood among the anxious mob, their swords clinking, lead balls rattling down musket barrels.

'What's the situation, lookout?' Blizzard called up to the man on top of the mast.

'She doesn't seem to be paying us much attention, sir,' the lookout cried back. 'She's got her stern to us. Travelling away, she is, sir!'

Dakkar squinted at the distant speck. In the dying twilight it was hard to tell, but he thought it was getting smaller.

Silence fell over the crew as they stood on the deck, willing the ship to vanish over the horizon. Finally, Blizzard snapped his telescope shut.

'Stand down, men,' he shouted. 'It looks like we struck lucky today!'

A relieved murmur spread among the sailors but Dakkar frowned and laid a hand on Finch's arm.

'What's that noise?' Dakkar said.

'What noise?' Finch replied, looking puzzled. 'Can't hear anything, lad.'

The noise felt familiar to Dakkar. A clicking and whining sound.

The whole ship shuddered and the crew fell silent

again. A hideous creaking groan rattled through the ship's timbers and suddenly the deck began to tilt.

Men scurried out of the hatches below, soaking wet, their eyes wide in terror.

'We've hit something, cap'n!' yelled one of the men. 'We're going down!'

The whole deck flew into chaos. Men scrambled to get the lifeboats down as the deck tilted even more. The port side of the ship began to vanish into the water.

'Come on, Dakkar,' Finch cried, clambering into a rowing boat.

But Dakkar could see a familiar shape moving down below in the water. And what *was* that sound?

Something hard punched him in the back and Dakkar spun round to see Slater's manic face above him.

'Nothing but bad luck, that's what you are!' Slater screamed, bringing his foot down hard on to Dakkar's chest.

Dakkar windmilled his arms but he couldn't stop himself stumbling backward across the slippery deck and he plunged headlong into the icy cold water.

CHAPTER TEN
EVIL TWIN?

Darkness had fallen completely now and the chill of the sea seeped into Dakkar's bones, numbing him. He shivered, treading water and listening for any clue as to where the lifeboats had gone. They had circled, the men rowing and Blizzard calling out names, but Dakkar's voice was nothing more than a hoarse croak. Every now and then, he heard shouts but they seemed increasingly distant. Here and there spars of wood drifted around in the eddying current left by the sinking ship. Dakkar grabbed one of these for support and rested against it.

I can't stay here for ever, he thought, his teeth chattering with the cold. *But which way to swim? I could end up swimming even further out to sea until I'm exhausted and . . .* He tried not to think what would happen when he ran out of energy.

He slumped over the rocking spar of wood and closed his eyes. The cold gnawed at him, making him ache all over. *Maybe I should just slip beneath the surface – swim to the bottom and join the fish. Then I wouldn't have to worry about Oginski. Perhaps I'd see Mrs Evans again.*

Tears stung his eyes as he thought of Oginski, of his parents at home not knowing that he was going to die. Dakkar blinked and stared down into the water. Deep beneath him a yellow light glimmered. It was moving!

Dakkar watched in amazement as the light grew closer. A cloud of silver bubbles boiled to the surface. He could see the black outline of a craft. *But the* Makara *sank,* he thought. *I saw it myself. There's no way she could return to the surface.*

The outline grew bigger. Dakkar's vision began to blur with the cold. In what seemed like a dream, light flooded the sea around him and he thought he could make out the shape of the *Makara* – only bigger, more streamlined. He kicked his legs, desperate to get some life back into them and to fend off unconsciousness.

With a hiss and a splash, the *Makara* bounced out of the depths and rocked on the surface.

It's a sea monster and it'll swallow me whole, Dakkar thought wearily.

A round hatch opened at the front of the craft and Dakkar was aware of a human outline and the golden light from inside flashing on glass lenses. But the cold and fatigue finally took their toll. Gradually he slipped off the beam that had kept him afloat and into the welcoming waves.

*

'Wake up!'

Something struck him hard across the face.

'*Wake up*, boy, or do I have to smack you again?' a voice snapped at him.

Dakkar's cheek stung. His clothes were still sodden with seawater and his black hair clung to his face. He opened his eyes and stared around at the unfamiliar surroundings. Except somehow he recognised exactly where he was.

He could see the wooden walls of the *Makara*'s lower cabin, the brass levers, wheels and handles. Fish drifted past huge portholes set into the polished sides of what could only be the *Makara*. Only it wasn't the *Makara*. It was too big.

A girl squatted in front of him. Freckles peppered her nose and cheeks. Her red, curly hair was tied in a wild ponytail, the fringe scraped back by a pair of goggles acting like a headband. She stared at him with sharp emerald eyes. Her long blue dress reminded Dakkar of the ladies bathing in the sea at Lyme Regis. But his eyes didn't linger on the girl for long. Instead, he blinked at the scene behind her.

Dakkar tried to sit up, only to find himself bound to the seat. 'What happened?' he groaned. 'And who are you?'

'I'll ask the questions here, boy,' the girl growled, an American accent giving her voice a nasal twang. 'Now where's my uncle?'

'Your uncle?' Dakkar spluttered. 'How would I know where he is? I don't even know who you are!'

'Don't make me slug you again!' she snarled, raising an

arm. 'You were on that British ship. Now where's Robert Fulton?'

'Fulton?' Dakkar felt the blood drain from his face. 'What d'you mean, where's Fulton?'

The girl swung her hand, stinging Dakkar's cheek. His eyes watered and he glowered at her.

'I said, I'll ask the questions,' she hissed. 'My uncle went for his usual constitutional walk in the evening, then I saw him being grabbed and dragged towards the sea.'

Dakkar noticed a purple bruise on the girl's temple. 'And you tried to stop them,' he guessed. 'Only they were too strong.'

'Too strong? Hah!' she said, folding her arms. 'One of them snuck up behind me and knocked me senseless. When I came to, I saw your ship on the horizon and launched the L–' She closed her mouth suddenly, swallowing her words and blushing slightly as if she'd said too much.

'This submersible,' Dakkar finished, unable to stifle a grin at her shock.

'How do you know that?' she gasped. 'You must be a spy. You *have* got my uncle.' She launched forward, almost sitting in Dakkar's lap, and started to bang his head against the back of the seat. 'Give him back, you good-for-nothing savage!' The craft rocked and tipped with the violence of her attack.

'I'm not a savage,' Dakkar yelled through gritted teeth. 'I'm not a spy either. Just stop and let me explain!'

Panting, the girl backed off and stared at him through narrow eyes. 'Go ahead then,' she murmured.

'My name is Prince Dakkar,' he said, catching his breath, 'son of the Rajah of Bundelkhand, in the province of –'

'I don't have much time for princes,' the girl snapped, raising her fist. 'We got rid of one king and don't need another.'

'I was staying with Count Oginski,' Dakkar added quickly.

'Oginski?' the girl repeated. 'I've often heard Uncle talk of him but I thought he was Uncle's friend.' She froze and her face flushed again. 'Wait a minute. You mean Oginski betrayed my uncle?' She leaned towards him, fists clenched.

'No, no!' Dakkar yelled hurriedly. 'Oginski has been taken too.' Dakkar's voice fell and tears stung his eyes again. 'They came in the night, killed Mrs Evans, our housekeeper. Oginski was working on a craft just like this one. He shared his notes with Fulton.' He gave a slight gasp as the realisation dawned on him. 'Your uncle must have been making a submersible at the same time as Oginski,' he said slowly. 'While your uncle built a sub on this side of the ocean, Oginski built one in England. They were building the subs and exchanging advice with each other but first Oginski was kidnapped and now your uncle.'

'A likely story,' the girl snorted. 'Why would my uncle share his ideas with this Count Oginski?'

'Think about it – you said yourself that they're friends,'

Dakkar replied. 'They're the greatest engineering minds in the world, so of course they would collaborate.'

'I don't trust you, *your highness*,' the girl said, jabbing Dakkar with her index finger. 'If your precious Oginski is missing, then what are you doing here with the Brits, kidnapping my uncle?'

Dakkar gave an exasperated groan. '*I* didn't kidnap your uncle! I thought the "Brits" on that ship had kidnapped Oginski so I went after them in *my* submersible – I called her the *Makara*.'

The girl sat quietly for a moment, chewing her lip. Dakkar could tell she wasn't convinced.

'So how come you were on board the *Palaemon*?' she demanded. 'And not in your . . . *Marraka*?'

'*Makara*,' Dakkar corrected, his face burning as he remembered how he lost her. 'I attacked a pirate ship and got caught in the wreckage. The sub sank and they rescued me.'

'You got caught,' she said, pulling a disapproving face at Dakkar. 'At least I can use the *Liberty* to good effect!'

'So you call this submersible *Liberty*,' Dakkar said, looking around. 'Was it you who sank the ship, thinking that your uncle was on board? Are you an imbecile?'

'Who are you callin' an imbecile?' the girl spat, and she jumped up, fists balled again.

'If Fulton was on that ship, surely he would have drowned by now,' Dakkar said, his voice cold. 'And you thought that sinking the ship was a good plan? You're lucky he wasn't aboard.'

The girl's face crumpled as she realised her mistake. Dakkar could see the worry lining her brow. Tears glistened in her eyes. She threw herself back in her seat.

'I know,' she said, sniffing back the tears. 'I was so angry but I didn't mean to hurt anyone. When the ship began to sink, I realised my mistake and panicked. That's why I came back. I was looking for survivors, anyone who might know anything.'

'I know how you feel.' Dakkar nodded, thinking back to when he almost rammed Blizzard's ship. 'But they didn't take your uncle.'

'Then where is he?' she sobbed. 'And who *has* taken him?'

'I don't know,' Dakkar said gently. 'But I bet it was the same people who took Oginski. Untie me and we can find them together.'

CHAPTER ELEVEN
THE BOATHOUSE

They sat in silence as the girl steered the *Liberty* through the waves towards land. Dakkar's cheek still tingled from the slap she'd given him. After some time she began to relax, and as she did she began to talk.

'My name's Georgia,' the girl said. 'Georgia Fulton. I live with my Uncle Robert. Aunt Harriet scolds him for showing me his inventions and all but I find it interesting. His own children are too young. The eldest is eight and not really interested yet. The girls are adorable though . . .'

Dakkar rubbed his face and pressed his fingertips against his eyes. *Does she ever shut up?* he thought. His wet clothes still clung to him and he felt chilled and shivery.

He scanned around the *Liberty* as Georgia rambled on. The sub looked incredibly similar to Oginski's version, only larger. The engine whirred at the back of the craft. A number of keys studded the surface of the control panel, each turning at a different rate. The central crank looked larger than the others and clacked as it whirled round. *It's clockwork too, like the* Makara *was.* Dakkar remembered the letters from Fulton in the *Makara*. They had compared notes closely. Dakkar recognised the lever for forward and back, the ballast wheel and even the auger in the roof.

'Is this how you sank the ship?' he asked, giving the auger wheel a twist.

'No, I just rammed her,' Georgia said, blushing. 'The *Liberty* has a steel spike in her nose. Was your sub, the *Maka-waddayacallit*, the same?'

'The *Makara*. Yes, but not quite as big,' Dakkar said. 'The small cabin of the *Makara* had a lid instead of this hatch.' Dakkar pointed to the hatch in the roof above the captain's seat. He felt a pang of loss and guilt. Oginski would have wanted the submarine destroyed and sunk rather than falling into enemy hands but, still, to have all that hard work just drift into the depths . . .

'It's more stable in the waves with just a hatch,' Georgia said. 'Uncle had a lid that lifted on an earlier boat but it tipped over. He nearly drowned!'

Dakkar gave a faint smile but for some reason he felt protective of his old craft. 'I'm sure Oginski had his reasons for not using a hatch,' he said, trying not to sound too defensive.

Georgia had stopped talking and was gazing intently at him. 'So,' she said. 'Tell me how you ended up on the *Palaemon*?'

As the engine whined, taking them nearer dry land, Dakkar told her about his escape from the castle and Blizzard. He didn't mention the fish-men. *You have to see them to believe them*, Dakkar thought. *She'd think I was mad.*

'What do we know?' Georgia said when Dakkar had finished his tale. 'Someone has kidnapped the two greatest inventors of our time, but who?'

'Apart from Oginski, did your uncle mention anyone else in connection with the submersible?' Dakkar asked her.

'No, but he did seem agitated these last few days,' Georgia replied. 'Maybe we can find some answers in the boathouse.'

'The what?' Dakkar said, frowning.

Georgia pulled on the drive lever and the engine quietened. Dakkar glimpsed the dark outline of trees as they glided up a woody creek. In the distance, a large rounded roof stood black against the moonlit sky.

'The boathouse,' Georgia explained, stopping the engine as the building loomed nearer. 'It was where Uncle Robert did most of his work. His papers are here too – most of them.'

Slowly the *Liberty* drifted into the shadow of what looked like a huge barn and they were engulfed by its darkness. Leaning up, Georgia popped the catches on the hatch and pushed it open.

'Are you going to tell your aunt and Mr Fulton's family what's happened?' Dakkar said, as he clambered out of the *Liberty* and on to the wooden staging that surrounded it on three sides.

'What? Oh no,' Georgia whispered, her face lost in shadow. 'There's no time. Whoever took my uncle is getting away. There'd be too much to explain. Plus they wouldn't let me go after him.'

'But they'll be worried,' Dakkar said.

'It sounds awful, I know, but they'll be worried either way so I'd rather not tell them,' Georgia said. 'Are you really a prince?'

Without waiting for an answer, she hurried to a small door at the back of the boathouse and disappeared through it. Within seconds, the glow of an oil lamp threw feeble yellow lines across the timbers of the boathouse. Dakkar heard Georgia rummaging and things being thrown aside. He crept up and peered inside.

The room was small and cobwebby. Boxes and cases lined its walls in a disorderly heap. Georgia had her back to Dakkar and was flicking through sheaves of papers.

Dakkar looked at the untidy desk with an aching heart. It looked so like Oginski's. A brown leather-bound journal, sitting on the edge of the desk, caught his eye.

'What's this?' Dakkar murmured, picking it up. 'Your uncle's diary?'

'We shouldn't read that!' Georgia gasped, putting a hand to her mouth.

'You said yourself that we don't have time to waste,' Dakkar said, raising his eyebrows and flicking through the pages.

Much of the diary outlined deliveries of materials and social appointments with the family. Boring details.

'Look at more recent entries,' Georgia suggested.

'Here, what's this?' Dakkar held the page up to the light and read aloud: '*Somehow my dealings with Lafitte have drawn the attentions of C. Had I known that the two did business together, I would have found another supplier, no matter how rare some of the components I needed proved to be.*'

'Lafitte?' Georgia gasped. 'Surely not!'

'Who is Lafitte?' Dakkar said, shaking his head.

'A pirate,' Georgia spat. 'He's wanted from here to the Bahamas! What would my uncle want with him?'

'It sounds like Lafitte was supplying goods to him,' Dakkar said, raising his eyebrows. 'If Fulton's anything like Oginski, he doesn't like to be too public about his inventions. Maybe this Lafitte was able to get things quietly with no questions asked.'

'I can't believe that Uncle Robert would trade with such a man!' Georgia whispered.

'Your uncle seems more concerned about this "C", whoever he is,' Dakkar said, turning the page over. 'Here, listen to this. *C's shadow grows longer. I saw something out to sea this morning that quite terrified me. From his letters, I can tell that Oginski is worried too. It may be wise to halt the submersible project and destroy what I have made. It would break my heart but if it fell into the wrong hands . . .*' Dakkar paused and looked up at Georgia. Her face was pale and she bit her lip.

'What does he mean about shadows and seeing something out to sea?' Georgia said faintly.

'I'm not sure,' Dakkar replied, thinking about the time he and Oginski saw the giant squid. 'But whoever this "C" is, he also deals with Lafitte. If we find Lafitte, then maybe we stand a chance of finding "C" and Oginski.'

'And my Uncle Robert,' Georgia added, narrowing her eyes.

'But where can we find Lafitte?' Dakkar said, slamming the diary down on the desk. 'He could be anywhere in the world!'

'No,' Georgia said, leafing through the papers again. 'Lafitte keeps to this side of the Atlantic, if the rumours I've heard are true.'

'It's still a large area to search,' Dakkar grunted.

'These letters here are bills of sale,' Georgia muttered, holding one up. 'They aren't from Lafitte.'

'Of course not,' Dakkar snorted. 'Pirates don't write out receipts!'

'No, but they'd use go-betweens, wouldn't they?' Georgia said, waving the paper. 'Mr Abercrombie Woolford-Potts, The Lime Tree Hotel, San Teresa . . .'

'San Teresa?' Dakkar said. 'That might be a place to start, wherever it is.'

Georgia scrabbled through another pile, pulled out a sea chart and rolled it open on the table.

'Here! It should take us three or four days to get to San Teresa Island,' she said, sweeping her finger across the map. 'We'll need food, water and spare clothing.'

She turned and hurried over to an old sea chest and began rifling through the contents. She scrunched up a red bathing dress and threw it behind her. It landed on Dakkar's head and he wrestled to pull it off. More clothes flew at him – trousers, undergarments – and he narrowly missed being hit by a boot.

'Put these in that trunk there,' she said, pointing to the corner. 'Here are some dry clothes for you.'

Dakkar felt his cheeks flush but he began to stuff the clothes into the trunk. Georgia stamped around the shed, grabbing tins and boxes from shelves and throwing them in. Dakkar sidled off into the shadows, dragged off his damp clothes and pulled on the dry ones. They hung loosely on him but weren't too oversized.

They must belong to Fulton, he thought.

Shafts of moonlight shone through the open door to the sea. Once the trunk was full, they dragged it down to the *Liberty* and manhandled it through the hatch along with two barrels of drinking water.

'Shouldn't we check we have everything we need?' Dakkar murmured, looking up at her from inside the *Liberty*.

'We'll be fine,' Georgia snapped. 'And what we don't have we can buy.'

As if to emphasise the point, she threw a bag down to him. Dakkar snatched it from the air and felt the weight of metal, the hard edges of coins through the leather. She clambered down through the hatch and squeezed past him into the captain's seat.

'Maybe I should go alone,' Dakkar said, putting his hands on his hips. 'It might be dangerous.'

'Do you want another pasting?' Georgia growled, wrinkling her nose. 'This is my uncle's ship!'

'I'm a prince of the blood,' Dakkar said, lifting his chin. 'It's natural that I should sail.'

'Are you gonna sit down or do I have to knock you down,' Georgia growled, '*your highness*?'

Dakkar stood for a moment but Georgia slammed the drive lever to *Backwater*, sending him into a crumpled heap at her feet.

'That wasn't funny,' he muttered, crawling into the passenger seat. 'You should show more respect.'

'You *earn* respect where I come from,' Georgia said, staring ahead. 'I'll need to sleep at some point and I guess you'll have to take over then, though where we'll end up I don't know. For now, shut up and let me sail.'

'Very well,' Dakkar growled back. 'Now, let's go.'

'Thank you,' she said, nodding to herself and reversing the *Liberty* out of the boathouse and into the creek. 'Here's the chart,' she said. 'Due south will do for now but we'll need to modify our course as we go. Can you navigate at sea?'

'Of course,' Dakkar muttered, hiding his face behind the crinkled map.

'And you want to be at the helm,' she said under her breath.

They sailed on in silence. The trees of the creek passed them and soon the water opened out. Georgia submerged the *Liberty* and the rough choppiness of the waves vanished. The engine whirred and clicked and Dakkar stared out into the empty sea.

Or was it empty? Dakkar peered harder through the glass portholes.

In the distance, something huge kept pace with the *Liberty*. Dakkar shivered. With its long trailing tendrils and a body that ended in a finned point, it looked horribly familiar.

CHAPTER TWELVE

WORSE THAN SHARKS

Dakkar kept a wary eye out of the porthole but the shape remained an indistinct outline. Soon the motion of the ship and the stubborn silence lulled him into drowsiness. He began to wonder if he'd imagined the shape. His eyelids felt like lead and, finally, he fell asleep.

Dakkar woke and jumped in his seat, wondering at the strange girl steering the submersible. His memory caught up with him and he breathed a sigh. He squinted through the porthole into the murky depths but couldn't see anything.

Georgia's head nodded wearily. She quickly corrected herself and widened her eyes.

'You're going to have to sleep sometime,' Dakkar said, his voice deliberately loud.

Georgia gave a start and then glowered at him. 'You gave me a shock . . .' She broke into an involuntary yawn and Dakkar suppressed a grin.

'I think you should let me steer for a while,' he said, sitting up straight. 'A good captain gives his crew responsibility.'

'You're right, I guess.' Georgia yawned and rubbed her eyes. 'But don't crash into anything, and wake me if something happens.'

'Of course,' Dakkar said through gritted teeth. 'Though you'll find I'm an expert sailor.'

'We need to wind the engine again,' she added, ignoring him. 'You turn all the keys. Multiple engines power the main one . . .'

'Ingenious,' Dakkar said, distracted by the intricacies of the engine. He turned the four keys and climbed down into the lower cabin to turn the main crank handle until it felt tight.

'The compass is housed in that box to the left of the wheel,' Georgia said, her eyelids drooping.

'Right,' Dakkar said, climbing back up to Georgia. He slid into the captain's chair.

Georgia clambered below, curled up on the small bed and within seconds she was snoring gently.

Dakkar grinned and gripped the wheel. *Let's see what she can do*, he thought. He rose close to the surface and extended the snorkel to let some fresh air into the craft. Then he sank again. Most of the controls were the same and in the same place. The front of the craft had four viewing portholes, which greatly improved visibility. He had to admit this was a much better version of the *Makara*.

*

The days rolled along with the tide. As they journeyed south, the sky became bluer and the air warmer. The squid didn't appear again and Dakkar put it from his mind.

Now he sat on the rim of the hatch, enjoying the calm and the sun on his face. Georgia sat at the helm below, poring over the sea chart. Dakkar took a breath and squinted across the blue horizon. This wasn't like the sea back in England. It was perfect. No land, no people to tell him what to do. For a few seconds, his troubles seemed so distant.

'What was that?' Georgia's voice called up from below, making him wince.

'What?' he snapped.

'Something just passed the porthole – something large and close,' she said.

Dakkar's breath hissed between his teeth. A triangular fin cut through the water ahead of the *Liberty* and the huge grey shadow beneath it told him all he needed to know.

'Shark!' he yelled. The fin veered left and circled back. Dakkar clambered over the top of the boat to track its progress. 'It's coming back.'

The fin passed just feet away from Dakkar as he scrambled for the hatch. But the boat rocked violently. With a cry, Dakkar's feet slipped from beneath him and he slammed on to the curved deck of the *Liberty*. Winded, he tried to scramble to his feet but gravity sent him sliding over the edge. The heat of the sun made the water feel cold and he gasped as he plunged in.

Floundering, Dakkar struggled for breath. The realisation iced his stomach: he was in the ocean and the shark was coming back.

Dakkar thrashed at the water, powering his way towards the *Liberty*. Clearly Georgia hadn't realised that she had lost him, and the gap between Dakkar and the craft widened.

'Georgia!' Dakkar yelled, the salt water making him splutter.

He glanced back. The shark was almost upon him. He could see the wave carved into the sea by the fin. The creature looked huge, its black button eyes fixed on him. Dakkar lashed out with his foot and felt his heel hit something rough and hard. The shark veered to one side, its black eyes rolling white, shying away from the sudden impact on its nose. But Dakkar didn't pause to celebrate. Water boiled in his ears as he plunged forward, desperate to catch up with the *Liberty*.

The shark appeared again, its red mouth framed by row upon row of serrated teeth. Dakkar twisted in the water and felt its rough skin skim his back. Gritting his teeth, he turned and jabbed his fingers into the shark's gills, gripping as hard as he could and punching at its eye. The shark thrashed its tail and plunged underwater, throwing Dakkar aside. The sea thundered around him and the blood pounded in his temples as he struggled to right himself.

With a gasp, Dakkar swam on. He saw Georgia's pale face through the front portholes of the *Liberty*. She'd seen him! But where was the shark? He risked a glance beneath and saw the bullet shape of the shark careering up towards him. Dakkar could see the cruel teeth again, the raw redness of its mouth.

The *Liberty* was inches away. He reached out, grabbing one of the brass handles that punctuated the side of the craft. With a yell, he dragged himself from the water and threw himself up towards the hatch.

The shark's gaping mouth filled his vision then it vanished. Thick red tentacles wrapped themselves round the shark's grey body as it thrashed from side to side just a few feet beneath him. Blood clouded the water as the giant squid's suckers cut into the shark's body.

'Get inside!' Georgia yelled.

Dakkar scrambled through the hatch and slammed it shut. He fell on to the floor behind her.

'Quickly,' he gasped. 'Full ahead!'

Blood and ink darkened the sea as Georgia sent the *Liberty* surging forward. Dakkar glimpsed a grasping tentacle, and then another, reaching from the dark cloud.

Suddenly the *Liberty* lost speed, jerking Dakkar and Georgia forward.

'It's caught us!' Georgia yelled.

The engine whined and groaned, battling with the pull of the squid. The extra weight of the creature sent them plummeting downward. The hull began to creak ominously.

'Do you have a friction machine?' Dakkar shouted.

'A what?' Georgia said, glaring at him.

'It gives an electric charge,' Dakkar snapped, wringing his hands. 'It's a crank wheel and a red button.'

'Yes, there!' Georgia pointed above her head. 'Why didn't you say that's what you wanted?'

Dakkar spun the handle as hard as he could. His body ached from his encounter with the shark but he managed to get twenty good turns and then jabbed the red button. The underwater world flashed blue and the portholes went dark as another cloud of sepia ink engulfed them. Dakkar's stomach lurched as the Liberty floated upward.

'Thank goodness for that –' Dakkar started to say but found himself flying forward, bent double over the seat in front of him. His head cracked against a porthole and he staggered back.

The tentacles of the squid thumped against the hull again. Georgia twisted the wheel sharply to the left, sending Dakkar stumbling across the cabin. His face pressed against the porthole and he saw the squid's suckered arms a glass-width from his face.

'It's pulling us down again!' Georgia groaned.

Dakkar whirled the friction machine wheel once more. His head pounded and he could feel blood flowing from his nose. He stabbed the button, sending a crackling charge into the water. The squid slid back and Georgia accelerated away, swerving the Liberty towards it.

'What are you doing?' Dakkar yelled.

Georgia gripped the wheel, her knuckles white, as the Liberty hurtled towards the squid. The squid threw open its arms as if to ensnare the craft. Dakkar dived into his seat as the sharp nose of the *Liberty* sliced into the centre of the beast. The huge eye stared and then was lost as the squid's razor-sharp beak opened. Dakkar was flung forward again. Blood and ink boiled in the water around them. The *Liberty* resounded with bangs and thuds as the squid thrashed out the last few seconds of its life.

Gradually the noise subsided as the squid drifted off the sub's nose and floated into the blue. Dakkar stared after it.

'It's missing an arm,' Dakkar whispered. 'It's the same squid that attacked Blizzard. I cut one of its arms off.'

'You're saying it followed us?' Georgia said, wide-eyed.

'I'm sure it's the same one,' Dakkar murmured.

'There can't be many squid that big,' Georgia said, her voice quavering. 'I hope not anyway!'

'At least the M– *Liberty* held up!' Dakkar said, smiling and giving the wall an affectionate pat.

Immediately a jet of cold seawater sprayed into Dakkar's face, sending him tumbling backward in shock.

The *Liberty* was letting in water.

CHAPTER THIRTEEN
GROUNDED

Dakkar stumbled forward and pressed his palms against the spray.

'Keep your hands against it,' Georgia said, and began to rummage at the back of the *Liberty*.

'Well, I wasn't going to let the water flow through and take a bath,' Dakkar grumbled. 'It looks like the squid did more damage than we thought.'

'Stand aside,' Georgia snapped. 'This should do the trick.' She pushed him out of the way and slapped a strange sticky substance over the crack.

'What's that?' Dakkar asked, peering closely at the grey mush.

'Some kind of clay,' Georgia said, smoothing it out. 'My uncle invented it.'

The spray stopped but the clay seemed to sweat, and droplets trickled down the inside of the craft.

'Will it hold?' Dakkar murmured, stepping back.

'For a while but we need to beach and repair it,' Georgia replied, grabbing the map and staring at it. 'We were lucky we were hit above the ballast compartments in the hull.'

'We'd better not submerge until we've fixed it,' Dakkar said, poking the clay.

'Don't prod it,' Georgia said briskly, and folded the map. 'There are no islands nearby. We'll have to head for the coast and try our luck there. You go up top and keep a lookout.'

'The squid killed the shark and we killed the squid,' Dakkar replied. 'Surely there can't be any other creatures out there!'

'How can you be certain of that? I'd be grateful if you'd oblige by keeping watch,' Georgia said, holding her head up. 'And don't mention it.'

'Mention what?' Dakkar said, frowning.

'Me saving your life.' Georgia grinned.

Dakkar felt his cheeks reddening. 'Saving my life?' he spluttered. 'You nearly left me behind! You didn't save me!' He turned and dragged himself out into the sunlight.

Despite what he had said, he scanned the sea for any fins or waving tentacles. It remained calm and serene.

Are all girls like this? he thought as he sulked on the curved deck of the *Liberty*. *I'll be glad when this is all over and I don't have to have anything more to do with her!*

He sat for an hour or so as Georgia steered the submersible. The sun dried his wet clothes as he stared out to sea.

Something grey and misty appeared on the horizon.

'Come and see this, Georgia,' Dakkar called down.

Georgia stopped the engine and they drifted as she clambered out of the hatch.

'I can see an island,' she said, peering through a telescope. Dakkar reached out but she snapped it shut. 'How strange that it isn't on the map. We'll head there anyway, see if there's somewhere to land the *Liberty*.'

The tiny island looked lost amid the vast blue ocean, a tuft of green poking up out of a desert of water. Its shape reminded Dakkar of a door wedge. At the high end, he could see a scrubby forest and a waterfall cascading from a cliff. The island sloped towards white breakers and foamy spray.

'It looks like we could anchor there,' Dakkar said, pointing to the narrow end of the island. 'But we'll have to watch that the sea isn't too rough. We don't want to be dashed against the rocks.'

Georgia steered the *Liberty* round the island and found a small shingly inlet on which to beach her. Dakkar and Georgia anchored the submarine and splashed ashore.

The pebbles crunched under Dakkar's feet and he gave a grin. 'It feels good to be on dry land again,' he murmured.

'I know what you mean,' Georgia agreed.

Dakkar felt a stab of annoyance. 'No, you don't,' he snapped. 'Apart from standing in your boathouse for a while, I've been at sea for weeks.'

'Well, we've been at sea for days since then,' Georgia tried to argue. She shielded her eyes against the setting sun. 'Anyway, it'll be dark soon. Any repairs will have to wait until tomorrow. We'll camp on the beach but we'll need some firewood.'

'And I'm supposed to go and find it, am I?' Dakkar snarled. 'While you rest here? I've been attacked by a shark and nearly drowned today, or had you forgotten?'

'Fine,' Georgia muttered under her breath. 'I was going to suggest we both went but if you're too exhausted . . .'

Dakkar watched her stalk off up the inlet towards the line of trees. *Maybe I should go after her*, he thought, but he stayed back, weighed down by hurt pride. He sat on the beach and listened to the swish of the tide, wondering if Oginski heard the same sound somewhere else.

Soon Georgia returned with an armful of dead wood and threw it down beside Dakkar. Then she strode back to the *Liberty*, returning with a tinderbox.

'There are breadfruit trees in there,' she said, not meeting his eye. 'We could boil some. It'd make a welcome change from salt beef.'

Dakkar gave a sigh and wandered off to the treeline.

The growing gloom of twilight deepened the shadows between the tree trunks. Dakkar shivered. Was there a movement in the darkness? A twig snapped and leaves rustled. Dakkar held his breath and crept forward. The undergrowth suddenly erupted, making him cry out as a flurry of brightly coloured birds squawked and flapped their way into the branches above. Dakkar blew out a sigh and laughed.

The breadfruit hung from the highest branches, requiring Dakkar to clamber up the trees. He was panting by the time he came back with a couple of decent-sized specimens.

A fire crackled on the beach and Georgia had set up a tripod and pan over it. Dakkar thought again of how ill prepared he'd been on the *Makara* and blushed at her efficiency.

'They look good,' she said, taking the breadfruit from him. 'I heard you cry out. Was everything all right?'

Dakkar gave a cough and couldn't help smirking. 'Just some birds,' he said. 'They almost flew into my face!'

Georgia gave a laugh and cut into the breadfruit with a long-bladed knife. Dakkar squatted and helped plop the chunks into the boiling water.

'I'm sorry I snapped at you before,' he muttered as they prepared the breadfruit.

'That's all right,' Georgia replied, giving a tight smile. 'Fighting sharks and gigantic squid doesn't put anyone in the best of humours.'

Dakkar laughed and relaxed a little. The breadfruit bubbled away and Dakkar realised just how hungry he was. The salt beef and weevily biscuits he'd been chewing on for the past few weeks had kept him from starving but the smell of something warm and fresh cooking made his mouth water.

Soon they were wolfing down hot chunks of the starchy fruit. Dakkar burned his mouth a couple of times but he didn't care. It wasn't long before the pan was emptied and the two of them were dozing by the fire with full bellies.

Dakkar shifted on to his elbow and stared at Georgia through the flames.

'So where did you learn so much about the sea and sailing?' he asked.

'My pa was a sailor,' Georgia said, blushing in the firelight. 'He doted on me. Taught me everything he knew.'

'You said "was". Did he retire?' Dakkar said.

'He died,' Georgia said, staring into the flames, 'fighting His Majesty's Navy.'

'Oh,' Dakkar said, suddenly feeling awkward. 'I'm sorry.'

'Anyway!' Georgia said, a false brightness in her voice. 'What's it like being a prince?'

'I don't know really,' Dakkar said, frowning. 'That all seems like another time, another life.'

'You've been away from home for a long time?' Georgia asked.

'I've been in England for at least four years. I ran away from a few schools and then Oginski took me on and I've kind of forgotten what it's like to be a prince.'

'You ran away from school?' Georgia said, wide-eyed.

'Well, it's hardly an adventure compared to this,' Dakkar said.

'No,' Georgia said, still agog at Dakkar's comment. 'I mean, what a waste! A good education is a real gift. I'd give my right arm to have proper school learning.'

'Believe me,' Dakkar replied. 'English schools are

neither proper nor are they a gift. They're brutal places full of bullying masters and hideous children.'

'Well,' Georgia said, 'I've no love for the English at the moment.'

'Now that's one thing we have in common,' Dakkar said.

'Do you think we'll find Uncle Robert and Oginski?' she asked quietly, changing the subject.

There's no doubt in my mind,' Dakkar said, his voice sounding brittle. 'We've just got to find Lafitte first.'

'And what if he won't help us?' Georgia whispered.

Somewhere in the distance a bird screamed at the night, and things scurried and scuffled in the woodland higher up the beach.

'Let's make the fire up,' Dakkar said, ignoring her question. 'We'll sleep on the beach tonight.'

Georgia rolled over and Dakkar threw more wood on to the fire. He watched the flames snap and flicker. More scurrying rattled the undergrowth and he peered into the darkness.

'I don't like this island,' he muttered.

But Georgia just snored in response, leaving Dakkar sitting, watching the dancing shadows.

CHAPTER FOURTEEN
A MYSTERY

The warm morning sun woke Dakkar from his sleep by the smouldering ashes of the fire. He groaned as he rolled over the shingle, shaking pebbles and fragments of shells from his hair.

When did I nod off? he wondered. He'd sat up for some time listening to the gentle whoosh of the sea – and the less comforting sounds from the woods behind him. But at some point he must have dozed off.

Georgia stood, flexing her arms and bending her legs, her red bathing dress flapping in the gentle breeze that blew in from the sea.

'Right,' she said, taking a deep breath. 'Let's have a look at the *Liberty*, decide what needs doing and then find what we need to make any repairs.'

'Did you hear any strange noises last night?' Dakkar asked her. 'From the woods?'

'Just birds, probably.' She grinned. 'Y'know, those

vicious ones that tried to kill you when you were collecting wood!'

Dakkar rolled his eyes and shook his head, then followed her down to the shoreline where the *Liberty* was lying on her side like a beached whale.

They ran their fingers along the overlapping planks, then Georgia went inside and tapped on the clay, identifying the location of the leak.

'Yes, that's it,' Dakkar called to her. 'I can see where the plank has been pushed in. It could have been a lot worse.'

Georgia's head popped round the prow of the sub. 'She's a tough one, all right!' she said. 'Do you think we can fix her?'

'It should be a case of a little tar on this side and keeping your uncle's clay on that one,' Dakkar muttered. 'If we can push the board out a bit that may help too.'

'There's a pot of tar in the back of the *Liberty*,' Georgia said. 'But it'll need heating. We'll need more firewood.'

'I'll get some,' Dakkar said.

'We'll go together,' Georgia said, flashing him a grin. 'But let's take some rifles with us.'

'Rifles?' Dakkar repeated. 'Your uncle included firearms in the *Liberty*'s equipment?'

'What's the point of arming the sub and not the captain?' Georgia said, wrinkling her freckled nose. She grew more serious. 'Besides, after yesterday I'm not taking any chances.'

With powder belts and rifles flung over their shoulders, they trudged up the shingle towards the treeline. Dakkar felt a mounting dread. It wasn't from anything obvious, just a bad feeling about the wood ahead of them.

'I feel as though someone is watching me,' Dakkar whispered, staring into the thick undergrowth. 'This place seems so odd.' He gazed above the trees at the rock that formed the highest end of the wedge-shaped island. This side of the rock rose up in a steep cliff face. 'Are those buildings up on the cliffs there?'

Georgia shielded her eyes with one hand and peered at the rock. 'They look like cave entrances,' she replied.

'Like square doorways,' Dakkar agreed. 'And why isn't this place on your map?'

'It's a tiny island.' Georgia shrugged. 'Hardly important. I guess it wasn't worth mapping out.'

'It'd be important if you ran aground on it during the night,' Dakkar pointed out. 'Or if you needed a beach to land on, like we did.'

They had reached the first scrubby undergrowth of the wood now and they began to snatch up any dead branches they could see. Georgia gave a snort of disgust and pulled her hand back. Her fingers were smeared in a greeny brown substance.

'Yuck!' she said, flicking her fingers away from herself. 'It smells like chicken poop!'

'It's big for a chicken.' Dakkar grimaced at the huge dollop that was smeared over the branches. 'And smellier!'

'It's truly foul,' she said, wiping her fingers on a broad leaf and then smiling when she realised her joke. 'Foul . . . fowl. D'you see?'

Dakkar rolled his eyes and carried on collecting firewood.

As they searched through the bushes, they found themselves climbing the hill towards the other end of the small island. Dakkar looked up at the square cave entrances.

'Now we're closer you can see they're man-made,' he said, pointing to the chisel marks. 'And look at the steps there.'

A narrow flight of stairs carved out of the rock wound up to the first row of caves.

'D'you think we should take a look?' Georgia murmured, but Dakkar had already put his wood pile down and was climbing up the steps.

The darkness inside the first cave blinded Dakkar for a moment. He paused, allowing his eyes to become accustomed to the gloom. It smelt musty and damp. Gradually, he made out the shapes of overturned boxes and chests, racks of cracked, cobwebbed bottles. Tables lay broken on the ground. A huge cage, its bars bent and twisted, stood in the corner.

'It looks like an abandoned workshop,' he whispered, picking up a bottle. 'I wonder who it belonged to.'

The crest on the sides of the crates showed a snake curling around a letter C with a trident poking up behind it.

'I've never seen a crest like this,' Georgia said, tracing a finger over it. 'What might it stand for?'

'Remember your uncle's diary,' Dakkar said, his eyes wide. 'He referred to "C".'

'The C could stand for anything though,' Georgia said. 'I wonder what this place was.'

They stepped into another room behind the workshop. More cages met their gaze, lined up like wounded soldiers, all wrecked beyond use.

'What lived in these?' Georgia said, tugging at the warped metal.

'Ask him,' Dakkar whispered, pointing.

Georgia stifled a scream. A skeleton lay in the corner of the room. He wore a black uniform and the fabric of the breeches was torn and ragged. His jacket bore the same crest as the boxes.

'He doesn't look to have died peacefully,' Dakkar said, gesturing to the pistol in the skeleton's hand.

He squatted down and gingerly pinched a thin slip of paper from inside the skeleton's coat. 'It looks like orders of some kind.' The paper crumbled in Dakkar's hands but he managed to read: '*Destroy all the specimens before they break free . . .*'

'Specimens – they're animals or things in a collection, right?' Georgia said, examining one of the cages. 'They must have been big.' She prised open a small barrel that lay next to the skeleton. 'And I betcha the next part of the orders was to blow this place sky-high.'

'Is that gunpowder?' Dakkar said, his eyes widening as he stared into the barrel.

'No, it's snuff.' Georgia laughed. 'Of course it's gunpowder! And look – there's more!'

Another barrel lay on its side by the door leading to the next cave. More bones lay scattered on the ground, belonging to four skeletons, judging by the skulls.

'Something must have torn them apart before they could blow the place up,' Dakkar gasped.

'I don't like this,' Georgia said. 'Let's get our firewood and get off this island.'

'I couldn't agree more,' Dakkar said, hurrying to the front cave.

But he stopped at the entrance. The trees that surrounded the clearing at the foot of the cliff swirled and thrashed about.

'Look,' Dakkar hissed. 'There's something down there. Something big.'

Lower branches swayed and snapped as whatever it was moved among the trees. Dakkar glimpsed white and black but couldn't work out what it was.

'Is it a big cat?' Georgia whispered. 'A tiger or a lion maybe?'

'On this island?' Dakkar said, smirking despite the strangeness of the situation. 'We're a long way from where lions and tigers roam!'

Suddenly the undergrowth shuddered and something burst out in a flurry of leaves and twigs. It squealed and yelped as it ran across the clearing at the foot of the cliff.

'It's a wild boar,' Georgia gasped. 'It looks terrified.'

More branches shifted and Dakkar saw a round eye, feathers and a cruel yellow beak. The creature's scream resounded across the island and into the cave.

'It's a bird,' Dakkar said. 'A huge bird. But I don't think it's the chicken you might have had in mind.'

The bird broke the cover of the trees and Dakkar caught his breath. It was immense, as tall as a large horse. A wicked, curved beak curled from a head that reminded Dakkar of an eagle. Stubby feathers stuck out of an ugly red neck. It bobbed, its yellow eyes fixed on the fleeing pig. Two huge legs powered the bird after its prey, long black talons scraping up chips of rock from the ground as it ran.

The bird's cry was echoed in the distance.

'I don't think it's alone either,' Georgia said, breathless.

With a flap of its stubby wings, the bird jerked its head forward. Dakkar gave a grimace as the sharp beak sank into the tough hide of the wild pig.

The boar squealed as the bird lifted it high in the air and then slammed it hard on the ground. For a second the pig lay stunned but as the bird threw its head up to cry out, it revived and scrambled to its feet. The bird snapped at it but the pig moved fast despite the gouts of blood that coated its back. With a squeak, it scampered across the clearing.

'It's going to get away!' Georgia gasped, grabbing Dakkar's arm.

But as the boar reached the edge of the clearing another black, feathered head flicked from the bushes. This second bird stood even taller than the first. It slammed a clawed foot on to the poor animal's back and pinned it to the ground.

Dakkar and Georgia watched in horror as the two birds tore their prey to pieces. They snapped and pulled, blood matting the short, stubbly feathers around their beaks. Soon only a dark stain on the rough ground gave any clue as to what had just happened. The birds stood, basking in the warm sun, preening and shaking their black and white feathers.

'That's what I heard screeching last night,' Dakkar whispered. He gave a shudder. 'And to think we slept out in the open.'

'Perhaps the fire discouraged them,' Georgia whispered back. 'But what shall we do now? Unless they move on we're trapped.'

'If they've just eaten,' Dakkar reasoned, 'then they might not be a threat to us. We could try to sneak past them.'

'Are you crazy?' Georgia hissed. 'Did you see what they did to that pig? They don't look like the sort of critter that ever stops being hungry.'

Dakkar nodded. One of the birds let out an unholy shriek and fixed a yellow eye on him as he leaned out of the cave. 'If we shoot, we might attract more birds,' he whispered. 'Stealth is our best tactic.'

They slung their rifles on their shoulders and climbed out of the cave on to the steps.

The birds lifted their heads but remained motionless.

Without saying a word, Dakkar and Georgia inched downward, step by step.

The nearest bird inclined its head.

Another step. They were five narrow stairs from the bottom now.

With a deafening shriek, the nearest bird launched itself towards them. Dakkar turned and stumbled on the bottom step. He fell flat on his stomach as the birds closed in.

CHAPTER FIFTEEN
THE TERROR BIRDS

Dakkar scrambled to his feet and leapt up the steps. He heard the clack of the sharp beak catching the cold stone where he had just been. With a yell, he threw himself forward two, three steps at a time until he reached the cave's mouth and Georgia dragged him in.

They lay breathless on the sandy floor, listening to the hiss and screech of the birds below.

'I guess . . . they're still . . . hungry,' Georgia panted, trying to catch her breath.

'Maybe . . . if . . . we could shoot them,' Dakkar suggested, crawling to the edge of the cave and pulling back the flintlock on his rifle.

'So much for stealth,' Georgia said. 'The birds are so huge, what if we only wound them and they run into the jungle? I've got a better plan.'

The birds were returning to the edge of the clearing

now, worrying at the roots of their greasy-looking feathers with their nasty, curved beaks.

She took one of the small barrels of powder and hurled it down into the clearing. The birds jumped and flapped, strutting towards the barrel and pecking at it curiously. After a moment's investigation, they went back to basking in the sun.

'Do you think this is wise?' Dakkar murmured as Georgia loaded one of the rifles.

'It'll frighten them away,' she said, taking aim. 'And we can run back to the beach.'

A loud crack lanced Dakkar's ear, followed by a buzz as the shot cut through the warm air. And then the clearing erupted into a roaring maelstrom of flame and smoke. Dakkar felt weightless for a second and then his head hit something. Stars splintered his vision and he wondered why he was lying at the back of the cavern, buried in boxes and rifles.

For a while an incessant whining filled his ears. He lay there, coughing out the stench of singed feathers and roasted flesh.

'Oops,' Georgia spluttered, crawling over to where Dakkar lay. 'I think I underestimated the amount of powder in that keg.'

Dakkar groaned and heaved a case from his legs. He stumbled over to the cave's mouth, nearly lurching out and falling headlong into the clearing.

A thin black mist still floated over the scene of devastation. Two smouldering carcasses lay at the edge of the clearing under the blasted undergrowth. A fire crackled on one side of the treeline and it was quickly taking hold.

'Just a suggestion,' Dakkar said, nodding at the ever-growing flames. 'But I think we'd better get back to the *Liberty*!'

'Good idea,' Georgia muttered.

They scrambled down the stairs, flinching at the flames that snapped at them from the bush. Dakkar could see that the fire was spreading rapidly.

'The path to the beach is still safe,' he yelled. 'We must hurry!'

As he finished speaking, a chilling screech filled his ears and he turned in time to see a flurry of black and white feathers come leaping over the flames and land right in their path. The bird was singed and charred from the flames but it was still dangerous. It stretched its neck out and gave a hissing scream at them.

'Another one?' Georgia whimpered.

Dakkar unslung his rifle and brandished it like a staff. 'You load up,' he said to Georgia. 'I'll try to hold it off.'

He could hear Georgia fumbling at her belt and loading her rifle but he didn't take his eyes from the bird.

'Quick as you can,' Dakkar said, parrying the bird's snapping beak with the butt of his rifle.

The bird lunged again. A stink of rotten meat drifted from the creature, cutting through the acrid smoke.

'I'm loadin' as fast as I can! Damn!' Georgia cursed behind him, and the sound of metal rattling on stone told him she had dropped a musketball.

Dakkar could feel the heat of the fire scorching his back now. He swallowed and swung the rifle at the bird's head. It made contact with a loud crack and the bird staggered drunkenly for a second. In another situation it would have looked comical, but Dakkar knew that with one lash of its powerful legs the bird could spill his warm guts on to the rocky ground.

It edged nearer and then reared up. Dakkar thrust the rifle butt out again as the bird brought its savage beak down. Pain lanced through his arm and then it went numb with the impact as he hit the beak. He dropped the rifle and stumbled back a little.

The bird did a tight circle back on itself and then began to run towards Dakkar. There was nothing he could do – his arm hung uselessly by his side. The bird gave a hop and extended the other leg, swiping its largest talon forward. Dakkar could see that its trajectory would bring it straight into his stomach.

Then another bang rang out almost right next to his left ear and a cloud of musket smoke choked him. The bird's head snapped back and Dakkar saw a gory hole where its eye used to be.

Although the bird was dead it still moved. Dakkar scurried to one side but crashed into Georgia. The bird's legs had lost their strength and buckled, sending it veering into them. Suddenly a mass of stinking feathers buried them, pinning Dakkar to the ground.

'I seem to be doing a lot of this,' Georgia grumbled, dragging at the dead bird's leg.

Dakkar struggled to his feet. His arm tingled as the feeling came back to it.

The flames grew higher, and further into the wood something crashed to the ground. The smoke thickened into a smothering fog. He snatched up the rifle and followed Georgia through the forest.

'And . . . don't . . . mention it,' Georgia panted.

'Mention what?' Dakkar gasped back.

'Me . . . saving your . . . life . . . again!' Georgia said, grinning.

Wild pigs scurried past them and smashed their way through the vegetation, desperate to escape the fire. Monkeys chittered and squealed above them in the high canopy. Brilliantly coloured parrots flapped and squawked through the leaves. Everything ran and flew to escape the heat and smoke.

Dakkar leapt over logs and stumbled on vines that snarled his feet on the ground. At one point a leopard hurled itself over his head. He even saw another of the giant birds stuck in the fork of a tree, snapping at anything that passed it.

At last the smoke thinned and the undergrowth lightened and he found himself staggering across the shingle towards the *Liberty* with Georgia. He threw himself on to the beach.

'Safe!' he cried.

'No – look!' Georgia yelled.

Flames still leapt from the trees and thick smoke obscured much of their vision but Dakkar could just make out a thin trail of smoke spiralling from one of the cave entrances.

'Sparks from the fire must have blown into the gunpowder barrels,' Dakkar gasped. 'But we're far enough away –'

'I didn't mean that,' Georgia breathed, pointing at the treeline. 'I meant *that*!'

Another giant bird was charging straight down the beach towards them, enraged, panicked and intent on destruction.

Dakkar tried to scramble to his feet but he slipped on the shingle. He was exhausted. His arms and legs ached with the exertion of running and fighting and being crushed by giant carnivorous birds.

'Load the gun,' he yelled at Georgia, who fumbled with the powder belt and the rifle.

The bird's curved claws kicked up the pebbles and grit as it sprinted towards them, head bobbing, beak gaping.

'I haven't got time,' Georgia grunted through gritted teeth. 'You'll have to fight it off.'

'I can't,' Dakkar screamed. 'It's moving too fast. It's going to jump and –'

The bird took a leap, spraying rock behind it. A muffled boom accompanied its take-off and Dakkar saw the caves behind it vanish in a huge cloud of black smoke.

CHAPTER SIXTEEN
SAN TERESA

As the bird reached mid-flight, stones rained down from the exploding cave, stinging Dakkar's head and forcing him to curl up tight. He glanced out from under the protection of his arm. The bird hung in the air but something else cast a dark shadow.

The bird twisted its head round and gave an outraged squawk as a huge slab of rock smacked it into the pebbly beach. Dakkar screwed his face up against the spray of stones, blood and feathers that enveloped him.

For a second, he knelt as if in prayer, motionless, staring at the rock that had buried the bird in front of him. Then he turned to Georgia, who stood with her jaw dangling slack at what had just happened.

'Does this kind of thing happen to you a lot?' he asked.

'What do you mean?' she said, frowning at him.

'Well, you know, going to fetch some firewood and ending up fighting off giant, man-eating chickens, being caught in forest fires and nearly getting crushed by exploding cliffs.'

'Erm, no,' she replied, dazed. 'I have had a few adventures but they don't generally involve giant, man-eating chickens, forest fires or exploding cliffs.'

'Oh,' Dakkar said. 'Me neither.'

Georgia broke into a smirk and then Dakkar felt a hysterical giggle force its way from the pit of his stomach. Soon the sound of their laughter echoed across the devastated island.

The submersible's repairs proved fairly simple. Georgia stood guard with all rifles and pistols loaded while Dakkar worked on the boat but they saw no more giant birds. Once they had made a fire to soften the tar that they needed to waterproof the *Liberty*, they were soon back at sea.

Dakkar manned the helm while Georgia consulted the charts.

'Our course is clear,' she said, running a finger along the map. 'But what we haven't thought of is what we do when we get to San Teresa.'

'What do you mean?' Dakkar said. 'We go to the Lime Tree Hotel mentioned in your uncle's letters and ask for Woolford-Potts.'

'And he'll lead us to Lafitte?' Georgia replied.

'With any luck,' Dakkar murmured. 'At least he might give us some idea where to look for him.'

'I've heard of this San Teresa. It sounds like a dangerous

place,' Georgia said, looking up from the chart. 'Full of cut-throats and thieves.'

'Then we'll have to be careful,' Dakkar said.

They journeyed on in near silence, their tension growing as the days sped by. When they did talk, it was to discuss the chart or compass readings.

The weather grew warmer and more humid. Sometimes they had to sail on the surface with the hatch open just to keep cool. At other times they would submerge but even under water the sun would warm the hull of the *Liberty*, making it hot and stuffy inside. They saw other ships and always submerged when they did so to avoid drawing attention. Dakkar felt a sneaking sense of power as the ships cut through the waves above, completely oblivious to their existence. Occasionally Dakkar would stare out at swirling shoals of silver fish. They saw plenty more sharks but none came near.

One day, Dakkar searched through the equipment in the *Liberty*. He found a long box in the lower cabin and opened it. Six spear-like poles, with fins at one end and wax globes at the tips, lay in the box.

'What are these?' he called up to Georgia.

'Oh, something Uncle Robert was working on,' Georgia replied. 'The globes are explosive, encased in wax for waterproofing.'

'What are they used for?' Dakkar asked, picking one up gingerly.

'Uncle Robert called them "Sea Arrows". See the

hatches on either side at the front of the craft?' Georgia said. 'You put them in there and press the button. Powerful springs fire them out and they explode on impact.'

'Why didn't we use them on the squid?' Dakkar said, placing them back gently.

'They're unreliable and the squid moved about too much,' Georgia explained. 'Better for buildings or maybe ships.'

Dakkar found many other weapons. The *Liberty* could produce an artificial sepia cloud like the squid's. Glass globes of ink were fired by a device at the back of the ship, giving it the chance to flee undercover. He found vicious-looking spikes that attached to the main ramming point. *The* Liberty *is far more warlike than the* Makara, he thought to himself but didn't share it with Georgia.

San Teresa looked to Dakkar as if a god had picked up a town and dropped it into a swamp. Peering through the telescope from the *Liberty*'s hatch, he could make out wooden dwellings with carved verandas and warehouses huddled together on the seafront. A jetty poked out into the sea and two ships were moored there. A ramshackle heap of shanty houses rose behind the main town. Trees and greenery sprouted between buildings and thick jungle reared up behind the whole town as if it wanted to push the houses into the ocean. The map had shown them that San Teresa nestled in the swampland deep in Barataria Bay.

'This is Louisiana,' Georgia had said, sweeping her finger around the map. 'That way's all swamp. There's

New Orleans. But this is where we want to be.' She stabbed at the map.

'Where can we hide the *Liberty*?' Dakkar asked, scanning back and forth across the island.

'Trust me,' Georgia said. 'These places are full of little creeks and inlets.'

They submerged and made their way to San Teresa, surfacing every now and then to establish their position and look for any inlets. Evening was falling by the time they found a suitable place.

'There,' Dakkar said, pointing from the hatch. 'It looks like we could anchor in that little bay.'

Georgia steered the *Liberty* into the inlet to find it led into a shallow creek. The boat's hull bumped along the sandy bottom and she brought the craft to a dead stop.

'Perfect,' Georgia whispered, climbing up and peering out. 'The narrowness of the creek means the vegetation overhangs us. The water will conceal us too. Let's go!'

'Erm,' Dakkar murmured, blushing. 'Do you think you'd better put something else on? The good people of San Teresa may be shocked by a young lady walking around in a bathing costume.'

'Oh!' Georgia stopped and glanced down at herself. It was her turn to blush. 'Yes, you may be right.'

Dakkar climbed out of the *Liberty*. A few minutes later Georgia followed, wearing knee breeches, a shirt and a cap that covered her long, red hair.

'A lady in trousers,' Dakkar said, feigning shock.

'I'll run around this town in a ball gown if you will, mister.' Georgia laughed as they picked their way through the undergrowth towards the lights of the town.

If San Teresa looked rundown from a distance, up close it was even worse. As they clambered through the trees, the smell of rotten food, rum and sweaty bodies hit them like a wall. The buildings looked ancient and weather-beaten. Sun-scorched and wind-blasted wood frontages with covered walkways lined the quagmire that was the street. Ragged-clothed beggars shook empty tin cups at every street corner. Tall, mustachioed men, armed to the teeth, swaggered through the crowds. Bar girls in silk, make-up and ill-fitting wigs screeched at each other and at the pirates from windows or saloon doors.

'This is the last haven for pirates,' Georgia whispered. 'The American Navy makes life pretty hard for them.'

'Keep a lookout for the Lime Tree Hotel,' Dakkar hissed back.

A fight broke out close by and a huge sailor in a sweat-stained jersey went sprawling into the mud in front of Dakkar. With a grimace he hopped over the groaning man and continued scanning the buildings. Somewhere, a fiddle struck up a tune and someone gave a cry of joy. Somewhere else, a musket shot cracked, making everyone in the street flinch and look around before continuing on their way.

'There it is!' Georgia said, pointing to a dilapidated corner building.

Dakkar curled his lip. If it were at all possible, the hotel lowered the tone of the street. Planks boarded up two windows and the garish lime-green paint on the front slats of the wooden building was peeling and cracked. An old man with no teeth and a long, grey beard lay snoring in the doorway, wrapped in a moth-eaten overcoat. His head hung back and his mouth was wide open.

'This is where Woolford-Potts lives?' Dakkar wondered aloud.

They stepped over the snoring old man and pushed the door open. Inside wasn't much better. A few characters propped up a long bar that ran the whole length of one side of the room. Bottles and barrels lay stacked behind the bar.

'What can I get yer?' the woman behind the counter demanded. Her red silk dress was faded like her blonde hair, which was greying and wiry.

'We're looking for a man called Woolford-Potts,' Dakkar murmured.

'Pay his drinks bill an' I'll tell yer where he is.' The woman extended a grimy, lace-covered hand.

'We don't have time for this,' Georgia said, scowling at the woman. 'We need to talk to him real quick!'

'Well, if you're in such a hurry,' the woman said, shaking her palm in front of them, 'then pay up and I'll tell yer.'

Georgia pursed her lips but dropped a silver coin on to the bar.

'He's been mighty thirsty lately,' the barmaid said.

Georgia dropped another coin. The woman scowled but picked the coins up and nodded over Dakkar's shoulder.

Dakkar turned round, following the barmaid's line of sight. Tables scattered with playing cards or empty glasses dotted the room. One man lay slumped over a table in the middle of the room, but over in the corner sat the roundest man Dakkar had ever seen.

The clothes he wore had seen better days and now stretched at the seams as the man leaned back in his seat, resting his hands on his huge belly. His ruddy face had an unshaven dirtiness to it and a white wig sat awkwardly on the side of his head.

'And to whom do I have the pleasure of speaking?' the big man slurred, his droopy eyes opening a crack as Dakkar and Georgia approached.

'My name is Georgia Fulton,' she said. 'I believe you have had some correspondence with my uncle, Robert Fulton?'

Woolford-Potts's eyes opened a crack wider. 'Fulton? Egad!' he said, and tried sitting up in his chair.

'You acted as an intermediary between him and . . . another person,' Dakkar said, inclining his head. 'We're eager to find that other person.'

Woolford-Potts's eyes widened even more. 'Not possible, I'm afraid,' he said, waving a chubby hand. 'I don't know what you're on about.'

'Look, Mr Woolford or Mr Potts, or whatever you call yourself,' Georgia said, her voice low and threatening. 'My uncle's gone missing and I've travelled a long way to find him. I think Jean Lafitte may be able to tell us where he is.'

'Shhhh!' Woolford-Potts was sitting bolt upright now and waving his hands. 'Be quiet – you never know who's listening. That man has many enemies who would love to get their hands on him.'

'Then you'd better start talking or I'll shout his name from the rooftops,' Dakkar said, raising his voice.

The men at the bar narrowed their eyes at Woolford-Potts and strained to listen.

'All right, all right!' Woolford-Potts hissed. 'But why do you think Lafitte may be able to help?'

'We think that he was working for someone else who was interested in my uncle,' Georgia explained. 'We think that whoever it was may have been involved in kidnapping Uncle Robert.'

'Oh no.' Woolford-Potts shook his head so vigorously that his wig slipped even further sideways. 'No, no, no. I can't help you. It's too risky.'

'So, Mr Woolford-Potts,' Dakkar said in a loud voice, 'how long have you been working with –'

'Stop!' Woolford-Potts moaned, dragging himself to his feet and then sitting heavily back down. 'I'll show you where Lafitte's hideout is.' He licked his finger and drew it through the grease on the table. 'This is the headland. This is Five Mile Creek. This is the biggest tree you've ever seen. It has a skull carved on it. Turn left here . . .'

The directions went on and Dakkar struggled to keep them all in his head. 'Haven't you got a map?' he said at last.

'I can remember it until we look at the chart back at the *Liberty*,' Georgia said, glancing over her shoulder at the men at the bar.

'I must warn you not to proceed with this,' Woolford-Potts said, gripping Georgia's hand. 'You're in grave peril.'

'I've faced pirates before,' Dakkar said, trying his best to sound confident.

'You don't understand,' Woolford-Potts said, his eyes wide. 'When your uncle approached me about smuggling certain items, the best person I could think of was Lafitte. But that other person you alluded to was also employing Lafitte. He was a jealous employer. He didn't like me muscling in at all.'

'What are you trying to say?' Georgia asked, frowning.

'It's not Lafitte you want to worry about,' Woolford-Potts said. 'It's the other man. It's –'

Something buzzed past Dakkar's ear. It wasn't a mosquito.

Woolford-Potts stiffened. A tiny dart poked out of the rolls of fat in Woolford-Potts's neck. He stared at them, eyes bulging.

'Cryptosssss,' he gasped, and crashed forward on to the table.

Georgia screamed and the men at the bar rushed over. Dakkar scanned the room but saw no one else. A sudden movement from the boarded-up window caught his eye.

'Grab them!' the barmaid screeched. 'They killed Potts!'

CHAPTER SEVENTEEN

MONSIEUR JEAN LAFITTE

The three men from the bar made a grab for Dakkar, who turned over the chair in front of him. They stumbled and tripped over each other, giving Dakkar a chance to dive to one side.

'Georgia, run!' he yelled as he bolted for the door.

The barmaid pulled a musket from beneath the bar. A huge bang shook the room, deafening Dakkar and sending the barmaid backward into her bottles and barrels. Plaster dust crumbled from the ceiling.

Georgia hurried after Dakkar out into the street, mingling with the crowd. A few curious glances were cast their way but then people pulled down their hats and moved on, not wanting to get involved.

'What happened to him?' Georgia gasped.

'I don't know,' Dakkar replied. 'It was some kind of dart. It came from the window but I couldn't see who fired it.'

'Do you really think he's dead?' Georgia panted.

'He didn't look very lively,' Dakkar said, dodging past a drunken old man with a crushed tricorne hat.

Dakkar kept glancing over his shoulder. Someone had been spying on them, following them. He didn't want to lead them back to the *Liberty*. Every face in the crowd looked suspicious. Each passer-by seemed to glare at them. They slipped into a side alley for a second and glanced back down the street.

'It looks clear,' Dakkar said. 'As far as I can tell.'

'What did Woolford-Potts say just before he . . . he . . .' Georgia couldn't bear to say it.

'It sounded like "Cryptos",' Dakkar replied, keeping an eye on the passing crowds. 'Maybe he's the "C" your uncle mentioned.'

They scurried on down the street and then ducked into the trees beyond the town.

'Wait here for a second,' Georgia whispered. 'We can tell if anyone is following us in these woods.'

They stood, hardly daring to breathe, listening for a snapped twig or a rustling bush, but heard nothing apart from the croaking of frogs and the chirping of crickets.

Reassured, they carefully crept to their mooring place and climbed into the *Liberty*. Dakkar reversed her out of the inlet while Georgia unrolled the map. She examined it, muttering under her breath and tracing their path with a trembling finger.

'That's it – round there, hard to port,' she said as they followed Woolford-Potts's directions.

'Do you think this Cryptos has Oginski and your uncle?' Dakkar asked her, staring into the darkness as he steered.

'It's possible,' Georgia replied. 'If Cryptos is the "C" my uncle was worried about.'

Dakkar gasped and stopped the *Liberty*. 'Look,' he said.

A huge tree grew out of the bank of the creek. Its roots twisted around themselves like snakes and dipped into the water. The white moonlight shone on a skull carved deep into the trunk of the tree.

'It can't be far now,' Dakkar said.

The trees and branches seemed to close in as they drifted on. At times the water became shallow and the *Liberty* scraped along the bottom of the creek. Leaves and branches split the moonlight into shafts of light that gave the place an eerie, unnatural feel.

Nightbirds broke the constant hum of insects, and every now and then something large would splash in the water under the trees.

A light in the distance told Dakkar that a cabin stood at the end of the creek.

'We'd better tie her up here and make our way to the cabin,' Dakkar whispered.

'You mean, swim in this water?' Georgia said, staring at him. 'There could be alligators in there.'

'Let's hope they're not hungry then,' Dakkar said, winking. But he swallowed hard as he climbed out of the *Liberty*.

Outside, the air felt sticky and hot. The smell of the swamp, of decay and sweetness, filled his nostrils. He lowered himself down the side of the *Liberty* and into the warm water. Something slimy slithered past his ankle and he stifled a scream.

'What's wrong?' Georgia hissed at him.

'Nothing,' he said, treading water gently. 'Just a fish, I think.'

Georgia splashed into the water next to Dakkar. He put his finger to his lips and then pushed off towards the cabin light.

'What was that?' Georgia groaned.

'What?' Dakkar said, frowning over his shoulder at her.

'Something slimy brushed past my leg,' Georgia whimpered. 'I really don't like this.'

'Oh, stop it,' Dakkar said softly. The water had become shallower here and he could stand up. 'Like I said, it's probably just fish or water snakes.'

'Water snakes?' Georgia's eyes widened. 'I do *not* like snakes.'

'I prefer them to pistols,' Dakkar said, staring straight up a gun muzzle.

A group of rough-looking pirates stood on the bank of the creek.

'Who have we here?' a dark, hawkish man said.

'Looks like kids, Martinez,' said another. This man was stocky with a straggly, grey beard.

'Looks like trouble to me, Renzo,' Martinez said, spitting into the water. 'Lafitte needs to know right away.'

Martinez nodded to Dakkar and Renzo offered a hand to pull Dakkar up. Georgia climbed up after him.

Dakkar weighed up the distance between Martinez and himself. If he made a sudden move, the pistol would blow a hole in him.

'Keep your hands up, lads,' Renzo said, producing his own pistol.

The third pirate, a thin, scrawny boy not much older than Dakkar, remained silent and followed them as they trudged towards the cabin. They stood on the veranda and the whole building rocked slightly. It seemed to Dakkar that the swamp was busy sucking the building back into itself. The planks were rotten and the curtains billowed ragged through broken windows. Martinez shoved Dakkar in the back and he stumbled through the flimsy wooden door, falling to his knees.

The warm and smoky atmosphere made Dakkar's eyes water as he was hoofed into the cabin. The interior was just as decrepit as the outside, with rotting plank walls, a sagging floor and vegetation encroaching through some of the gaps in the walls. Lafitte's men sat at the worn wooden tables and looked up in surprise at Dakkar and Georgia. Some even leapt to their feet, hands gripping the hilts of daggers.

Dakkar clambered to his feet, rubbing his skinned knees. He glanced over to meet Georgia's glowering eyes.

'And who or what do we have here?' said a heavily accented voice behind them.

Dakkar turned. A short dark-haired man sprawled in a high-backed wooden chair, leaning his pointed chin on his bejewelled knuckles. His rich red tunic and fine-leather knee-high boots marked him out as the leader of these ragged pirates.

'Children, Jean,' Renzo said, waving a hand at Dakkar and Georgia as if he were a magician and had just conjured them up.

'Imbecile!' Lafitte snapped, straightening in his seat. 'I can see they are children! Where did they come from?'

'We found 'em in the water,' Martinez said, his eyes widening. 'They were sneaking up on us.'

'Sneaking up on us?' Lafitte echoed. He jumped out of the chair and stared up at the hulking pirate. 'All two of them?'

'Uh, yeah,' Martinez muttered, breaking eye contact with Lafitte.

'It's a good job I put you on watch, Martinez,' Lafitte sneered. 'Anyone else could have been overpowered by such overwhelming odds!'

Laughter rippled among the other men as Martinez stood there looking in bewilderment from Lafitte to Dakkar.

The pirate captain turned to face Dakkar. 'What are you doing here?'

'I am an American citizen and demand that you treat me accordingly!' Georgia said, her cheeks reddening.

'The last "American citizen" I met was the captain of a navy frigate.' Lafitte grinned as he paced around her. 'He went overboard to talk to the sharks. Perhaps you are spies, sent by the American government.'

'Do we look like spies?' Georgia snorted. Her neck was red now as she glared at Lafitte.

'In my experience, mademoiselle,' Lafitte said, smirking, 'spies seldom look like spies!'

'They're just little ones,' Martinez murmured, recovering from Lafitte's joke at his expense.

'Nevertheless, they could have been sent by the navy,' Lafitte said, squinting at Dakkar. 'Nothing surprises me with these Americans.'

'S'il vous plaît, monsieur,' Dakkar said, stepping forward. Georgia stared at him wide-eyed and Lafitte's eyebrows arched in surprise as he continued in fluent French. 'We mean you no harm. We have come here seeking my guardian and this girl's uncle.'

'You speak like a Frenchman,' Lafitte replied in the same language. 'Where are you from?'

'My name is Dakkar. I have travelled from England, sir,' he replied.

'You speak French well for an Englishman and yet you look like no Englishman I've ever met,' Lafitte said. 'You could be from India or the Far East. Who is it that you seek?'

'I'm looking for my mentor and guardian, Count Oginski,' Dakkar said, trying to meet Lafitte's gaze.

Lafitte pursed his lips. 'Oginski,' he said simply, and looked at Georgia. 'And you, my dear, what is your uncle's name?' he said in English.

'It's familiar to you,' Georgia said, narrowing her eyes. 'Robert Fulton. You worked for him last year.'

'Maybe I did, maybe not,' Lafitte said, shrugging. 'But why have you come to me if you're looking for them?'

'Because we think that someone you know might be interested in them,' Dakkar said. 'Does the name Cryptos mean anything to you?'

The men around Lafitte gave a collective hiss and shuffled back an inch or two.

'That name upsets my men, mon ami,' Lafitte said. 'Choose your words carefully or I cannot vouch for your safety. You think this Cryptos has taken your precious guardians?'

'We do,' Dakkar said hastily. 'But at the very least he may be able to help us find them.'

A strange look of horror and amusement twisted Lafitte's dark features. 'Then we should make you as comfortable as possible,' he replied. 'And see if we can help you find him. We're all very helpful around here, eh, mes amis?'

Lafitte gave a grin and looked around at the pirates. They responded with a horrible chuckle.

'Martinez,' he continued, 'could you show these two to the guest rooms?'

'Yes, Lafitte,' Martinez said, leering at them. 'Come this way.'

Frowning, Dakkar followed Martinez, with Georgia close behind. They crossed the dilapidated room and Martinez threw open another door. It was dark and dank inside but empty.

'What's this?' Dakkar began, but a sharp kick sent him sprawling into the room and Georgia landed on top of him, winding him.

The door slammed shut, leaving them in pitch blackness. Dakkar groaned and rolled over.

'Georgia?' he said, squinting into the dark.

'I'm here,' she whispered. 'But I don't think much of Lafitte's guest room.'

'It's nothing personal, mes amis,' Lafitte called through the door in French. 'You wanted to meet Cryptos? Well, I suspect he might want to meet you too. I've heard rumours he's been hunting for someone and I think I can turn a dollar or two out of it.'

Dakkar launched himself at the door but it proved surprisingly robust considering the rotten wood from which it was made.

'Save your energy.' Lafitte laughed. 'You'll need it when I sell you to Count Cryptos!'

CHAPTER EIGHTEEN
THE WRATH CHILD

Dakkar hurled himself at the door once again. Pain lanced up his shoulder but the door didn't budge. He staggered back on to the floor and groaned.

His eyes became accustomed to the gloom and Dakkar saw Georgia's pale, worried face.

'We're trapped,' she whispered, 'but maybe it's not such a bad thing. I mean, Lafitte is taking us to Cryptos, after all. That's what we want, right?'

'I'd rather meet him on my own terms, not shackled and delivered like some prize,' Dakkar muttered, searching the floor and walls. Finally, he gave a hiss of triumph and pulled at a vine that poked its way through a tiny crack in the corner of the room.

Outside, the talk had become louder, more raucous. Someone played an accordion and sang for a while. Dakkar could hear the clink of tankards as the men drank.

'Let me help,' Georgia said, hurrying over to Dakkar and pulling at the vine.

Gradually the crack widened. Rotten wood crumbled away in shards but the hole was only big enough for them to get their arms through. Dakkar grabbed the edge of the floorboards with both hands and listened to the ebb and flow of the singing and talking.

'I know this song,' he whispered. 'There's a chorus coming – it might be loud enough to cover the sound of this plank coming up.'

The singing reached a crescendo. Some men shouted and banged their tankards on the tables. Dakkar heaved at the plank. With a crack, the nails popped from the joists beneath. He could see the ground below. He paused, waiting to hear the door opening or the alarm being raised, but the tuneless wailing continued. Another chorus came up and Dakkar pulled again. Another board popped.

'Now, quickly, through the hole and underneath the cabin,' Dakkar said.

Georgia slipped into the darkness and he followed her silently.

The ground under the cabin felt damp and thorny. Dakkar bit his lip as he dragged himself through the undergrowth. Footsteps thumped above his head and the singing droned on. It dawned on him that the cabin sat on an island in the middle of the creek. Bridges from one patch of dry land to the next had brought them there once they had been caught.

Dakkar slid into the water at the side of the cabin, pressing his finger to his lips as he noticed Martinez and Renzo on the veranda, grumbling to each other.

'This is the second watch I've had to do in three days,' Martinez said, kicking the side of the cabin. 'And every time a night watch.'

'Me too,' Renzo sighed. 'And I love a good sing-song.'

'Maybe they don't like your singing.' Martinez laughed.

Keeping to the edge of the creek and crouching in the water, Dakkar and Georgia slipped past the two pirates. Soon they had made their way back to the *Liberty*.

'What now?' Georgia muttered. 'We're no nearer getting to Cryptos.'

'No, but Lafitte knows where he is,' Dakkar said, pulling the hatch down and climbing into the captain's seat. 'We just need to persuade him to tell us. And stealth is *not* the best tactic for that.'

'What are you going to do?' Georgia gasped.

'Load up those Sea Arrows.' Dakkar grinned. 'We're going to put the *Liberty* through her paces. I'm really angry now.'

Dakkar turned the *Liberty* on and slammed her to *Full Ahead*. The motors whined and she began to accelerate. Bushes and branches whipped past. Something banged heavily against the hull and flew into the undergrowth. A flock of birds exploded from the trees, disturbed from their night rest.

'We'll crash!' Georgia screamed from below. 'You can't destroy the *Liberty*.'

'The *Liberty* rammed a British Navy frigate and sent her to the seabed,' Dakkar snarled. 'With enough speed, she'll easily ride the bank of the creek and smash Lafitte's shack.'

'You're mad,' Georgia said faintly.

'Absolutely! I'm tired of asking questions and getting no answers,' Dakkar yelled. 'I'm tired of sneaking around and I'm tired of pirates. Now fire, Georgia!'

Dakkar heard Georgia thump the buttons at the side of the *Liberty*, first one then another. A comic *boing* cut over the whirr of the engines. Dakkar saw the arrows glisten in the moonlight. He saw Martinez, wide-eyed and open-mouthed. He saw Renzo dive headlong into the water. And then the swamp lit up fiery yellow as the two arrows exploded into either side of the cabin.

The cabin rocked in the blast, wobbling from side to side like a jelly. Dakkar gripped the wheel until his knuckles cracked, and he screamed at the top of his voice. The shack grew nearer and nearer, filling the port-holes. Pirates leapt from windows and doors as the *Liberty* ploughed through the creek towards it.

A loud *whump* reverberated through the *Liberty* as she skipped across the water like a flat pebble sent spinning by some giant child. Dakkar flew up out of his seat, banging his head against the roof as the speed of the *Liberty* sent her up on to dry land.

The doorway of the cabin cracked and splintered as the *Liberty* crashed through the flimsy wooden structure. The world was filled with the rending of wood and the creaking of timber. Dakkar glimpsed Lafitte standing slack-jawed amid the carnage, and then the back wall came screaming at him. Another bang took the *Liberty* through the rear of the shack. She landed with a splash back in the water on the other side of the tiny island. Pirates floundered in the shallows, staggering around in disbelief.

Dakkar grabbed the friction machine wheel, wound it ten times and stabbed the red button. The swamp was lit up blue this time and Dakkar watched as Lafitte's men slumped into the water like puppets with their strings cut.

Not wasting a second to explain, Dakkar leapt up and out of the hatch. He slid down the side of the *Liberty*, splashing through the water and across the island to where Lafitte stood, dazed. He still held the handle of his shattered tankard in his hand. The beer stained his once-fine tunic.

Recognition washed across Lafitte's slack features as Dakkar charged towards the pirate. Lafitte dropped the tankard handle and fumbled at his belt for his pistol. With a yell, Dakkar swung his fist. The pirate's bristly chin scratched at Dakkar's knuckles and the shock of the blow numbed his arm. A sharp right followed the left blow and then Dakkar brought his leg in a high swinging arc into the side of Lafitte's head. With a muffled groan, Lafitte tumbled to the ground.

Dakkar grabbed the pirate's collar, dragged him back through the ruins of his shack, into the water and up to the side of the *Liberty*.

Georgia stood on the deck, her hands to her face.

'Oh my,' she said as she surveyed the smouldering wreckage of the cabin surrounded by the twitching and moaning remnants of Lafitte's crew. 'Remind me never to cross you.'

'Hurry!' Dakkar hissed. 'Help me get him inside the *Liberty* before they come to their senses.'

Georgia grabbed Lafitte and helped Dakkar manhandle him up to the top of the craft. He wasn't a tall man – maybe an inch taller than Dakkar – but he was stocky, and once they had him at the edge of the hatch they let him go. The pirate fell with a heavy thump straight through both hatches and into the lower cabin.

'Oops!' Georgia giggled, leaping in after him, her cheeks flushed with excitement. 'I'll tie him up. You get us outta here!'

Dakkar grinned back, slammed the hatch shut behind him and bounced into the captain's seat. He steered the *Liberty* round the wrecked island cabin, knocking over a few dazed pirates on the way. A musket cracked, its bullet whizzing close by a porthole. Dakkar pushed the *Liberty* to *Full Ahead*, drenching the stumbling pirates in his wake.

'Where d'you learn to fight like that?' Georgia called up from below.

'My father taught me,' Dakkar replied. 'A prince should always be able to defend himself.'

'Well, I guess you did that all right!'

Dakkar gave a tired grin, rubbed his aching shoulder and set a course for the open sea – and Count Cryptos.

CHAPTER NINETEEN
THE MYSTERIOUS ISLAND

'What makes you think I will help you find Cryptos?' Lafitte snarled, straining against the ropes that pinned his arms to his sides.

He looked a mess. Swamp water and spilt beer stained his clothes and he had a bruise on his forehead where Dakkar had knocked him out.

'Georgia!' Dakkar called up from the lower cabin.

'Right,' Georgia replied, and turned the submerging wheel.

'Mon Dieu!' Lafitte bellowed as the *Liberty* began to sink beneath the waves. 'We are sinking! What kind of devilry is this?'

'You've seen what the *Liberty* can do, monsieur,' Dakkar said. 'Now will you help us or will you go for a swim out there?'

'Very well,' Lafitte growled, narrowing his eyes at Dakkar. 'But you must untie me.'

'No,' Dakkar said, sprawling a sea chart over the table. 'We'll let you go when we get to Cryptos. Now show me where he is.'

'This is so undignified,' Lafitte grumbled, shuffling over to the map. 'If we ever meet again, I will make you pay for this humiliation. But that is unlikely.'

'What do you mean?' Dakkar said.

'Few people meet Cryptos and live to tell the tale,' Lafitte sneered. 'I hope he boils you in oil.'

'Who is this Count Cryptos?' Dakkar said.

'He is a devil,' Lafitte said, the colour draining from his face. 'A ruthless killer. I don't know what he wants with your precious friends but I doubt that they still live.'

'We don't know for sure that he has them,' Georgia muttered from the captain's cabin above.

'So where is he?' Dakkar asked, changing the subject.

'Here.' Lafitte pointed to the map as best he could. 'A small volcanic island, a day's sail from here.'

'We'll be there in no time,' Dakkar said.

'This is a truly wonderful machine,' Lafitte said, staring around. 'Imagine what a pirate could do with such a craft.'

'I shudder to think,' Dakkar said, glaring at the Frenchman.

'Did your friends make this boat?' Lafitte asked.

Dakkar shrugged.

'If they did, this will be the reason Cryptos has them,' he declared. 'And this may be why he is looking for you also.'

Dakkar pursed his lips and took the chart up to Georgia, who set the *Liberty* in the direction of the island.

They travelled in silence for a while. Every now and then, Lafitte would curse and test his bonds.

'Look, why don't you untie me?' Lafitte said finally. 'My arms are numb and I can't do anything anyway – we're under the sea.'

'I don't think so,' Dakkar said, curling his lip.

'Please,' Lafitte said, his voice rising. 'I swear I won't try anything. What could I do? I do not know how to sail this machine.'

Georgia looked at Dakkar for a moment and then nodded.

'Very well,' said Dakkar. 'But any tricks and we'll sink to the bottom of the ocean and you'll be trapped there.'

Dakkar untied the ropes and Lafitte swung his arms and stamped his feet.

'You would do well to find a way to get on to his island by stealth and cunning,' Lafitte said. 'I'm sure Cryptos has many guards and defences.'

For some reason, Dakkar thought of Oginski's castle and the caves in the cliff. 'We could explore the perimeter of the island underwater first,' he said, peering at the map. 'Maybe there are tunnels or caverns we could use.'

Georgia submerged the *Liberty* further, much to Lafitte's great consternation. He pressed his face against the glass porthole and peered up at the surface. But soon he was crying out in wonder as dolphins or a sea turtle swam by. Once he swore he saw a wreck deep below them and the glitter of gold. As the journey wore on, he fell silent, watching the undersea world pass by. In the end he dozed off, and Dakkar felt it safe to sleep too.

'Well, we should be here,' Georgia announced as she brought the *Liberty* to the surface. 'We just need to check we're in exactly the right place.'

'Bon!' Lafitte declared, and began to climb the ladder for the upper cabin. 'I will leave you here and swim ashore.'

He stopped abruptly as Georgia pushed a pistol against his nose.

'Sorry, monsieur,' Dakkar said, holding out the rope. 'But I think we should tie you up again.'

Lafitte grumbled but extended his hands for Dakkar to bind his wrists.

The *Liberty* bobbed up through the mass of bubbles and Dakkar peered through the portholes. In the distance, he could see a tendril of smoke trickling upward from a cone-shaped peak. Dense jungle clustered around the volcano, finally giving way to rocky beach.

'It doesn't look inhabited,' Dakkar muttered, wiping the condensation from the glass.

'Believe me,' Lafitte murmured over Dakkar's shoulder, 'the devil himself lives on that island.'

'We have to believe you,' Georgia called down from the captain's cabin. 'But, I swear, if you've taken us on a wild goose chase, you'll be looking in from the other side of that porthole.'

'I'm sure of it!' Lafitte said, pulling a face at Dakkar.

'We'd better submerge and see if there are any caves or tunnels we might use to get into the island,' Dakkar said, turning away from the view and indicating to Georgia that they should submerge.

Dakkar couldn't stop marvelling at the beauty of the seabed. Multicoloured fish danced in and out of huge banks of coral while seaweed swayed with the tide.

They skirted the island, getting closer and closer.

'What's that?' Georgia called out.

Dakkar peered through the larger portholes of the lower cabin. This side of the island rose in a series of plateaux, like a stepped mountain, from the seabed. And a huge cavern entrance gaped in the side of the steps.

'Let's see what's in there,' Dakkar said quietly. Suddenly it felt very warm in the *Liberty*. A bead of sweat trickled down his back.

'Do you think it is wise, mes amis?' Lafitte whispered.

'I don't know,' Dakkar replied. 'But we're about to find out.'

Georgia steered the *Liberty* towards the cavern entrance. Dakkar couldn't help thinking about the fishmen he'd seen in the castle cave. They were a distant memory after all that had happened since then.

Georgia gasped. Clusters of stalactites and stalagmites lined the cavern's entrance like rows of wicked teeth. Strange, brown coral twisted its way around the rocks, mottling the walls.

'It looks like a huge mouth,' Georgia said, shuddering as they drifted nearer.

Dakkar scrambled up next to her and peered through the gloom. There was something not quite right. A few air bubbles drifted up from the corner of the entrance. The seaweed didn't grow out of it so much there as around the edge.

'Pull back,' Dakkar snapped.

The stalactites were close now, sharp and pointed. They weren't jagged rock. They were bone.

'What?' Georgia said, frowning at him. 'But we –'

'It *is* a huge mouth!' Dakkar yelled, snatching at the wheel and sending the *Liberty* careening to port. 'Pull back now!'

At that same instant, the whole side of the cliff moved and the cave mouth widened. Two glowing eyes appeared through a cloud of swirling mud as a massive fish snapped down its teeth. Georgia screamed and rammed the lever to *Full Ahead* as the teeth grated down the polished wooden side of the *Liberty*.

'Mon Dieu,' Lafitte exclaimed from below. 'It is some kind of monster.'

The colossal fish had obviously lain in the entrance to the cave, blocking it completely with its open mouth. Waiting. Dakkar could see its flattened, lumpy body, the bony fins lashing the water as it powered after them.

Georgia spun the wheel again, throwing Dakkar against the wall of the submersible. From below, they could hear Lafitte's curses as he crashed about in the lower cabin.

'Imbecile!' he bellowed. 'Are you trying to kill me?'

But the fish darted after them still, its glowing eyes filling the rear portholes.

'It's gaining on us!' Dakkar yelled.

'Use the sepia bomb,' Georgia said, twisting the wheel again and sending the *Liberty* into a spiral that brought more curses from below.

Dakkar slid down the steps and opened the box containing the glass sepia globes. Two round brass hatches dotted either side of the back wall of the craft. He slid one open and pushed the glass ball in, then repeated the procedure.

'Is this spring-loaded like the Sea Arrow mechanism?' he shouted up to Georgia.

'Yes, wind it and press the button,' she called back through gritted teeth. 'Only, do it quickly. This thing's gonna take a chunk out of our tail!'

Dakkar wound the crank next to the sepia hatch and Lafitte copied him, cursing at the ropes that restricted his movements. Then Dakkar jabbed his thumb against the button and scrambled up to see if it had worked.

A brown cloud boiled in the water behind them, obscuring everything.

'Uncle Robert mixed the sepia with an acid solution,' Georgia explained, swinging the *Liberty* to face the fish as it emerged from the cloud of ink. 'Its vision should be impaired now.'

'Sea Arrows?' Dakkar suggested.

Georgia grinned and nodded.

'This is a formidable craft,' Lafitte panted as he loaded

a dart into one of the tubes. 'The man who created it must be a genius.'

'He is,' Dakkar replied, loading a second missile. Then he corrected himself. 'They are!' He fired the arrow and peered out of the lower portholes.

Georgia had put the *Liberty* into reverse as the arrows had fired in order to escape as much of the explosion as possible. One arrow flew past the fish but the other struck home as the creature thrashed through the water towards them. A flash dazzled Dakkar and the surge of the blast rocked the *Liberty*, sending him and Lafitte staggering from side to side, bumping into each other.

'Again I find myself on my derrière!' Lafitte snapped as he landed on his backside.

Dakkar scrambled to the porthole. The sepia mist was thinning to reveal the smouldering bulk of the fish as it sank, trailing a growing cloud of blood.

'The entrance is clear now,' Dakkar said, peering beyond the sinking remains.

The cave stood open, waiting for them.

'What if there are other such terrors lurking within it?' Lafitte said, becoming pale.

'Then we'll deal with them,' Dakkar said as Georgia powered the *Liberty* through the gory cloud of blood towards the cliff.

An uneasy silence fell over the *Liberty* as she crossed the threshold of the cave. Dakkar could see scales and fragments of coral where the fish had lain in wait. He suppressed a shudder and then gave a gasp.

The darkness of the cave gave way to a curious fluorescent light emitted by hundreds of glowing jellyfish. They drifted like ragged candelabra, a pulsing green and blue halo around each one. The columns and pillars of volcanic rock reaching up from the cavern floor reflected the eerie light, dancing with shadows.

'They're beautiful,' Georgia whispered, dropping the wheel to stare out.

'I've never seen anything like it,' Lafitte whispered in French.

But Dakkar stared beyond and between the trailing fronds of the jellyfish. Dark shadows weaved in and out. Man-shaped shadows. Every now and then the light would shimmer on a scaly back or reflect on a milky eye. They had company.

CHAPTER TWENTY
CRYPTOS

'There are people out there,' Georgia whispered, staring through the porthole into the illuminated cavern.

'Sirènes,' Lafitte gasped.

'What?' Georgia said, frowning at Lafitte. 'Will you please speak English?'

'Since when did you Americans speak English?' Lafitte snapped, waving a dismissive hand.

'Mermaids,' Dakkar said. 'Though not the fairytale kind. These have legs, not fishtails.'

'And they are not as beautiful as I have been led to believe,' Lafitte said, pouting his bottom lip.

A scaly body flashed past the porthole, making Georgia scream.

'I've seen these before,' Dakkar said. 'They were in the pool when I first set off in the *Makara*.'

'You never mentioned it.' Georgia scowled at him.

'I wasn't sure I believed it myself,' Dakkar murmured,

peering out. 'They attacked me last time but they're keeping their distance now.'

'They must have seen the devastation this thing can wreak,' Lafitte said, not taking his eyes from the fish-men.

'They're guiding us,' Georgia said, shivering as two fish-men crossed in front of the *Liberty*.

Dakkar could see their huge pearly eyes and drooping mouths now. Loincloths of seaweed clung to their muscled legs and waists as they kicked with webbed feet away from the *Liberty*. The fish-men swam ahead, sweeping the water with their powerful arms, and gradually a channel formed in the mass of jellyfish. Dakkar stared in wonder at the pulsing wall of light as they followed.

'Well, so much for sneaking up on Cryptos,' Dakkar said, shaking his head at the sight outside.

'Should we go back?' Georgia asked, pulling a face at her own suggestion.

'I don't think we can,' Dakkar muttered. 'There are hundreds of fish-men out there. Besides, these creatures were at the castle, which suggests that Oginski will be here too.'

'They are swimming to the surface,' Lafitte said.

A sheer rock face loomed in the distance, marking the furthest edge of the cavern. Georgia emptied the ballast tanks and, slowly, the *Liberty* began to rise after the fish-men.

The scene above the surface was as breathtaking as that below. Above the light of the glowing water huge columns of rock rose high into the shadows. Pinks and greens shimmered on the walls until they vanished into the darkness. In the distance, across the cavern, shafts of dusty daylight broke in through several entrances. The sound of waves crashing echoed through them.

But what took Dakkar's breath away was the craft that lay at the side of the pool. The sea lapped on to a small wooden dock that jutted from a rocky ledge, and lashed to this jetty was a huge submersible. A massive tube, it was almost as long as Blizzard's frigate, with a tower in the centre of the hull. With its polished wooden boards and brass, it shone in the half-light of the cavern.

'It's incredible,' Dakkar gasped.

'Do you think Uncle Robert and Oginski built it?' Georgia said.

But Dakkar could make out human shapes standing on the jetty. As they drew closer, fish-men leapt from the water and grabbed ropes to secure the *Liberty*.

Out of the water, the fish-men looked more or less human in shape. A fine sheen of scales coated their skin. Some shimmered green, others blue. Knots of green hair flowed down over their shoulders. The pouting lips and large glassy eyes gave them a look of sadness, which was exaggerated by the strange catfish barbel that hung like a moustache from the corners of their mouths.

'I can see people,' Georgia said. 'Is it Uncle Robert?'

'I don't think so,' Dakkar replied, slipping down to the lower cabin and heading for the exit hatch.

The *Liberty* bumped and banged as she was pulled

alongside the landing stage behind the huge submersible. Dakkar could see the name *Nautilus* engraved on a brass plate on her hull.

Lafitte lifted his bound wrists in front of Dakkar. 'The least you could do is untie me,' the pirate said. 'I have done what you asked of me. This could be dangerous and I may need to defend myself.'

Dakkar paused and chewed his lip. He couldn't trust the pirate but he had a point.

'Very well,' Dakkar said, pulling a knife from his belt and cutting the ropes round Lafitte's wrists.

Georgia appeared behind Dakkar and they looked at each other. She handed him a loaded pistol.

'Ready?' Dakkar said.

Georgia nodded. Lafitte gave a mocking bow and a flourish with his hands towards the ladder that led up to the hatch. Dakkar shook his head, indicating that he should go first. His heart pounding, Dakkar clambered up after him.

The warmth of the air in the cavern struck Dakkar first – that, and the smell of sulphur. A tall, gaunt figure sat in an ornate sedan chair, flanked by six fish-men, their milky eyes glowering, fins fanning the air at their necks. The man gripped the chair's arms with thin fingers that ended in incredibly long, sharp nails. He wore silk robes that were so black they seemed to flow down into the smooth, glassy floor. A drooping moustache exaggerated the length of his pale face and the glow from the water gleamed on his bald head. Dakkar would have taken him for a Chinese nobleman but his sad blue eyes gave him away as European.

'Welcome, your highness,' the man said, nodding to him. 'It is an honour indeed to meet you at last. I am Count Cryptos, ruler of this humble island abode.'

The blood pounded in Dakkar's temples. The last time he had seen that slender figure, heard that voice, it had held the lifeless body of Mrs Evans.

'You! I'll make you pay for what you did,' Dakkar snarled, taking a step towards Cryptos. 'Where is Oginski?'

'And my Uncle Robert?' Georgia added, pulling the pistol from her belt.

The fish-men either side of Cryptos hissed and leaned forward, ready to spring at them. He waved them back.

'All in good time,' Cryptos said, his voice sounding distant and melancholy. 'The death of Oginski's house-keeper was regrettable, Dakkar, but you will come to understand that, in the grand scheme of things, a few lost lives is the price we pay for greatness.'

'Her name was Mrs Evans and she was a sweet, harm-less old woman,' Dakkar growled, clenching his fists. 'You killed her for no reason.'

'I can see that Oginski has infected you with his senti-mentality while you have been in his care,' Cryptos sighed, shaking his head. 'But when you learn the truth you will see who is right.'

'What are you talking about?' Georgia snapped, raising her pistol.

'Please, Miss Fulton, put the pistol away,' Cryptos said,

holding his hands up. 'All will become clear. Your precious uncle is quite safe, as is Oginski – for now. However, the Qualar despise firearms and would cheerfully drag you into the water for brandishing such a weapon.'

'Qualar?' Dakkar said, frowning and signalling for Georgia to put the gun away. 'These fish-men?'

'Ah! Fish-men, how quaint,' Cryptos said, smiling. 'And accurate, in a way. The Qualar are our undersea cousins, Dakkar. They breathe through gills and have lungs too. The Qualar, people of Qualarium – a great civilisation that is now under my control!'

'You're just plain evil,' Georgia snarled.

'We can trade insults later, my dear,' Cryptos said. He smiled and gestured to the *Nautilus*. 'You haven't remarked on my other creation here. I copied the design from your uncle but he and Oginski have been helping to finesse it.'

The sound of the *Liberty*'s hatch slamming shut cut Dakkar's retort dead. He turned to see Lafitte staring triumphantly from the porthole then glance down at the controls with a frown. Dakkar ran back as the engine began to whine, kicking up water from the stern of the craft.

'Don't trouble yourself,' Cryptos said with another sigh. 'The craft is still tied to the jetty. My Qualar will extract Lafitte from the submersible and he can join my workforce.'

Realising he was going nowhere, Lafitte gave a sheepish grin and shrugged through the porthole.

'I want to see Oginski,' Dakkar demanded.

'And you will, my dear boy,' Cryptos said. 'But you have a lot to learn. For now, my guards will escort you to your chambers. We will all meet later.'

He clicked his long fingers and the Qualar lifted the sedan chair to their shoulders. At the same moment, more Qualar came slithering out of the water to form a line between Dakkar and Cryptos.

'Wait!' said Lafitte, poking his head out of the *Liberty*'s hatch. 'Your worship! Count Cryptos! I brought these children to you – I should be rewarded!'

'I'm sparing your life,' Cryptos said without turning his head. 'I'm giving you the chance to work for me. Be thankful I don't feed you to my jellyfish.'

'Oh,' Lafitte called after him as Qualar dragged him back out on to the jetty. 'Then, thank you, your greatness.'

'If you'd helped us instead of trying to trap us, you might be in a better position,' Georgia spat, and stamped on Lafitte's foot.

A Qualar guard pushed her along the jetty. Dakkar followed, giving Lafitte a dark look as he passed.

'You're all devils!' Lafitte called after them. 'How is a man expected to make an honest living with fiends like you blowing up his house and home?'

But Dakkar wasn't listening. They entered a ragged doorway cut into the wall of the cavern and walked up a steep passage. More tunnels snaked off this main walkway. The whole volcano was honeycombed with shafts. Qualar marched back and forth, carrying boxes and sacks. Some were armed and clearly on guard duty outside heavily riveted doors. Human guards in black uniform accompanied them.

'Look,' Dakkar said, nodding at the crest on their jackets – a snake curling around a letter C and a trident poking up behind it.

'The same badge as on the skeletons we found at the other island,' Georgia said.

'It must have once belonged to Cryptos,' Dakkar added. 'Like this place.'

'It's a maze,' Georgia whispered to Dakkar.

'And a fortress,' he hissed back.

Burning torches flickered in brackets along the smooth walls, casting an eerie, dancing light on the scaly green faces of the guards. They stopped at a thick wooden door.

'Give weapons,' one of the Qualar said in a gulping voice.

Dakkar took the knife and the pistol from his belt and handed them over.

'In here,' another Qualar said.

He opened the door and Dakkar stepped into a sumptuously decorated room. Colourful tapestries hung from the walls. A bed with a thick mattress filled one corner, next to a writing table and chair. A huge tank full of fish lined a whole wall.

'But where will Georgia –' Dakkar began, but the door slammed in his face and a key turned in the lock.

Dakkar threw himself at the door. It was too late. He was locked in.

CHAPTER TWENTY-ONE
SECRETS

Dakkar sat on the bed and took a deep breath. He wanted to scream, to grab the carved chair and smash it through the fish tank. But that wouldn't help. *Anger has no eyes*, he thought. His mother used to say that. It meant that when you're angry you're careless. *Use your eyes, Dakkar!*

He crossed the room to the door and peered through the keyhole. *It would be simple to pick*, he thought, scanning the room for anything he could use as a tool. Oginski had taught Dakkar how many things worked, and encouraged him to dismantle objects. Old locks were the first things on which he worked.

Two lamps gave light to the room – one hung from the wall, the other stood on the table. The handle of the oil lamp on the table was composed of several strands of thick wire curved round from the base to the lid. Blowing the flame out, he wrapped the lamp in sheets from his bed to protect him from the heat and slammed the lamp to the floor. The handle snapped at the second attempt. Dakkar smoothed one of the strands out and approached the lock.

The light was dim now and Dakkar held his tongue between his teeth as he concentrated on teasing the levers in the lock casing. In the distance, he could hear a metallic clunking and a strange roar echoed through the keyhole. Dakkar shivered. Suddenly the lock gave a click and he pulled the door open a crack.

The corridor looked clear. Cryptos had underestimated him.

Sidling along the wall of the passage, Dakkar listened. *Where is Georgia?* Should he follow the metallic thumping sound? More doors dotted the walls of the tunnel. He decided to try one of these and reached for the next door handle.

The room behind the door lay in darkness. The feeble light from the torches in the corridor outside cast a rectangle of light into it. Dakkar could make out some bars but it was the eye-watering dung smell that hit him first and made him pull his head back. As he did, a roar deafened his ears and huge leathery fingers whipped the air in front of him.

A massive gorilla towered over Dakkar. It gripped the bars of the cage and rattled them angrily, baring its yellow fangs at him and banging its forehead against the cold metal. Dakkar backed out, slamming the door shut.

'Giant creatures,' Dakkar murmured, thinking back to the island of the terror birds.

He crept further down the passage and came to a set of

rough stairs. Footsteps echoed down the corridor. Dakkar scanned from left to right, searching for somewhere to hide. He even considered running back to the gorilla room. A narrow tunnel opened on to the passage just above him. He jumped, grabbing the lip of the entrance, and heaved himself up. He just had time to drag himself into the narrow vent before two human guards strode by, rifles at the ready.

A hot breeze blew over Dakkar, bringing with it the metallic thumping he'd heard before. An eerie red glow illuminated the far end of this narrow passage. Gasping with the effort, Dakkar managed to turn himself round and crawled along towards the sound and light.

It must have been a natural vent hole, Dakkar thought. Debris littered the ground and it was so narrow his back brushed against the top. The drop at the other end broke his train of thought as he nearly crawled out into open air.

Dragging himself back into the vent, Dakkar looked out over the chamber below. The vent exited from a sheer wall a hundred feet up from a glassy floor. Somewhere high above, a circle of daylight cut through the shadows. This was the top of the volcano.

In the centre of the chamber stood a colossal machine. It was a massive cylinder, short and squat and standing on four metal legs. Attached to its base was an enormous corkscrew cone. Qualar seethed across the chamber, carrying sheets of plate metal. They clambered all over the machine using ropes and ladders, lifting their metal to workers at the top, who hammered and riveted them in place. They reminded Dakkar of insects scurrying all over a carcass.

It looks like some kind of digging machine, he thought, staring at the monstrosity that dominated the room.

In among the workers, Dakkar could see the odd ragged human, staggering under the weight of his load. Other Qualar and black-uniformed human guards stood at the sides of the room or at the base of the ladders. They held spears and guns. Some cracked whips at workers who stumbled or staggered. Clearly not all inhabitants of Qualarium were willing servants of Cryptos.

Dakkar watched for a while, trying to guess the exact nature of the machine. All the time, his attention was drawn to the brutality of the guards, beating and whipping any who fell behind.

Having seen enough, he scrambled back along the tunnel, his breath sounding deafening in the confined space. Slowly, he lowered himself into the main passage and made his way onward, passing more doorways as he went. Some were storerooms, silent and still, but others concealed growling creatures. He glanced through barred windows, hoping to find Georgia or Oginski.

The tunnel climbed gradually and came to a solid metal door. Dakkar could hear raised voices from behind it. Creeping closer to the door, he pressed his ear to the metal. It felt cool against his cheek.

'Please, if you have the boy, then let me see him,' said a deep, rumbling voice.

Dakkar recognised it instantly. *Oginski!* He made to push at the door but the next voice sent a shiver down his spine and he froze.

'When the Mole is finished and I have what I want,' Cryptos said, 'you can spend all eternity together. Unless the boy chooses to stay with me, of course.'

'He would never do that,' Oginski snarled.

'Even when he learns the truth?' Cryptos said.

The truth? About what? Dakkar pushed the door open and peered through the crack. Oginski stood in the middle of a large hall. It reminded Dakkar of his father's throne room, where merchants and peasants alike would come to beg for favours or mercy. The sedan chair had been set down at the end of the long room and other chairs stood around a table big enough for a great feast. It was richly decorated but Dakkar barely noticed the details as he stared at Oginski.

The big man had lost some weight but still had an impressive presence. Worry lined his face and his sleeves were rolled up as if he had been working on something.

Cryptos stood across the room, flanked by five Qualar guards armed with sharp spears and swords.

'I don't believe Dakkar is capable of the evil you want to teach him,' Oginski said, clenching his huge fists.

Cryptos heaved a sigh. 'Franciszek,' he said wearily, and it sounded strange to Dakkar to hear Oginski's first name spoken out loud. 'Frank, my brother. Is it evil to want to bring peace to this troubled world? To free people? To throw down despots?'

'Throw down?' Oginski spat. 'Only to put yourself in their place.'

But Dakkar wasn't listening any more. *Brother? Cryptos called Oginski his brother?* He remembered the pirate's story. *Is it true?*

A cold metal point pricked Dakkar's shoulder, making him yelp and stumble forward. A Qualar guard had crept up on him and now stood behind him as Dakkar fell into the room, crashing the door open as he went.

Cryptos's guards leapt forward. Two levelled spears at Oginski's throat while two put themselves between Cryptos and Dakkar.

'Dakkar!' Oginski whispered, his face full of emotion.

'Ah! Your highness.' Cryptos smiled, regaining his composure quickly. 'I am impressed. I hadn't expected you to escape so quickly.'

'Dakkar. What are you doing here?' Oginski hissed. 'I told you to go back to your father, not to look for me.'

'How could I do that?' Dakkar said, his heart sinking. He wanted to give Oginski a hug. To say how glad he was to see him safe. 'You were kidnapped. Mrs Evans, she . . .' Dakkar could feel tears burning the back of his eyes. 'I thought Blizzard had taken you. I chased his ship but . . .'

'You should be congratulating the boy,' Cryptos cried, shaking his head. 'He has overcome impossible odds to get here. He showed a ruthless determination. A single-mindedness that once you would have been proud of, my brother.'

'It is true,' Oginski said, acknowledging the question

in Dakkar's eyes. 'This is Kazmer Oginski, my brother. Though the years have changed us in different ways –'

'Yes,' Cryptos interrupted. 'You have forgotten the evil that brought us to this place. The deaths of our mother, our father and the beauteous Celina, all at the hands of a Russian tyrant. We made a vow to avenge ourselves on all nations that impose their will on others. A vow that you quickly forgot.'

Oginski lunged at Cryptos, only to be grabbed by the guards and held tight in their grasp.

'I never forgot,' Oginski said through gritted teeth. 'I just sickened of the pointless slaughter.'

'We railed against the world at first, Dakkar,' Cryptos said, shaking his head sadly. 'We drowned our sorrows in a sea of violence. Once the vow was made, we went our own separate ways. I became a pirate, striking terror into the fleets of the world's nations.'

'You became a monster,' Oginski cut in.

Cryptos inclined his head. 'Maybe,' he said. 'But the brothers met once more. We all realised the futility of our actions. Why fight alone when together we could be a formidable force? Why face the limitless power of the enemy on the battlefield when we could fight covertly? When we could stab in the dark and flee? And so "Cryptos" was born. I am Count Cryptos but so are all my brothers. So is Oginski here.'

'Never!' Oginski yelled, and lunged again.

'Kings love their flags and trumpets, their pomp and ceremony,' Cryptos sneered, turning to Dakkar. 'But sometimes it's better to be nobody, Dakkar – unknown, unnoticed, until the last, fatal moment. We will strike at the heart of nations and they will never even know what killed them.'

'But why?' Dakkar asked, his heart thundering.

'Why?' Cryptos smiled. 'Because the rulers of the world's great nations are corrupt. They're happy to squabble and fight in endless wars. We will stop all that. We will unite the world under our leadership. But to do that we must tear down the so-called civilisation that already exists.'

'You will kill millions of people,' Oginski said, struggling to break free.

Again, Cryptos inclined his head in agreement. His eyes looked sad, almost tearful, to Dakkar.

'That is true,' Cryptos said. 'But the sacrifice will be worth it when we live in peace and prosperity.'

'You're mad,' Dakkar gasped. 'There are just six of you. Even with a small army, how can you change the world?'

'It only takes one man to change the world, Dakkar,' Cryptos said, fixing him with an intense stare. 'I've bred an army of giant creatures. You saw my first unfortunate mistakes when you visited my previous island stronghold. I was particularly proud of those terror birds but they were hard to control. Yet here, with the help of the Qualar, I've amassed a mighty force. What fleet could stand against a shoal of giant squid? What army could fight creatures that mindlessly do my bidding?'

'You set that monster on Blizzard's ship,' Dakkar said, staring at Cryptos. 'You sent it to attack me, didn't you? And the giant crab at the castle was your doing.'

'Tests for both you and the creatures. My Qualar have been shepherding them towards you throughout your odyssey. But our plans go far beyond the brute force of such beasts,' Cryptos sneered, striding across the room and pulling back a curtain. 'And I think you'll be willing to help me.'

Dakkar gave a gasp. Three large glass tanks were set into the wall. Strange eel-like creatures swam over and under each other in the first. They were thick and black, squirming around in the slimy green water that filled the tank. The second tank held a man, ragged and scorched. Dirt smudged his face and his long, grey beard. He pressed his calloused hands against the thick glass. In the third, glowering in the corner, sat Georgia.

CHAPTER TWENTY-TWO
CHOICES AND THREATS

Before Dakkar could say a word, the door banged open and two more guards dragged a man into the throne room. He looked a younger man than Oginski, with a head of thick, curly brown hair and a pointed nose. Where Oginski stood tall and muscle-bound, he stooped slightly, carrying a lot of weight around his middle.

'Uncle Robert!' Georgia cried, jumping up and hammering on the glass.

'Georgia?' Fulton gasped, peering through his glasses into the tank and then glancing at Cryptos. 'What's going on? What is my niece doing here?'

'How touching,' Cryptos sighed as Fulton tried to run at the glass only to be restrained by the Qualar guards. 'Your niece came to rescue you, Fulton. She shows spirit. I admire that in anyone.'

'Let her go!' Fulton demanded.

'No,' Cryptos said, strolling over to the glass tanks. 'Oh, don't worry. I won't harm her, just as long as you cooperate.'

'We've helped you build the *Nautilus*,' Oginski said, narrowing his eyes at Cryptos. 'What else would you have us do?'

'You don't fool me, Oginski. I know you've been looking for ways to use the *Nautilus* to escape. Why else would you cooperate with me? No, my eye is on a bigger prize. Deep below the sea that surrounds this island,' Cryptos said, running a finger down the glass, 'lies the Eye of Neptune, an ancient source of unlimited power.'

'That sounds like hocus-pocus,' Fulton sneered. 'Tribal legends? I thought you'd be more rational than believe in that, Cryptos.'

'I believe that the Eye is a Voltalith,' Cryptos said. 'Oh, that got your attention, didn't it?'

'What's a Voltalith?' Dakkar said, frowning at Oginski.

'A fragment of rock that holds a static charge,' Cryptos cut in before Oginski could answer. 'I believe the rock is from deepest space. It crackles with electricity.'

'But we're engineers,' Fulton said, shrugging. 'We know nothing of electricity.'

'You're a brilliant natural philosopher, Mr Fulton,' Cryptos said, smirking. 'But you're a poor liar. Both the submersibles you built had devices that electrocuted attackers. You know enough to help me harness the power of the Eye of Neptune. Once it's cut into smaller pieces, it will power a whole fleet of submersibles and drive all manner of machines.'

'Why don't the Qualar get it for you?' Dakkar demanded.

'The Qualar are a superstitious race. Their fear of it is even greater than their fear of me,' Cryptos said with a shrug. 'On a more practical note, any living thing that goes near the Eye dies a horrible death.'

'Then you could use that *Nautilus* craft to get it,' Dakkar countered.

'It isn't quite ready,' Cryptos said. 'Your little craft will do the job nicely, with a few modifications.'

'So you want to use the *Liberty* to get this Eye of Neptune?' Dakkar said, his arms folded.

'You've proven yourself to be an adept captain,' Cryptos said, smiling. 'If you collect the Eye of Neptune for me, Georgia will remain safe.'

'The boy can't go,' Oginski burst out. 'I'll do it.'

'Prince Dakkar will go,' Cryptos said. He tapped on the glass and pointed to the bedraggled man in the glass tank. 'This man here tried to escape from my mines on the island. He will provide us with an accurate demonstration of what will happen to Georgia if you do not do as I say.'

Cryptos pulled a lever in the wall and the glass partition between the man and the eels slid up. The man's eyes widened and he slammed his fists against the sides as water and eels sloshed into his tank.

'Technically speaking, they aren't eels,' Cryptos said, sounding mildly surprised. 'They're a kind of fish found in the swamps of the southern Americas. Observe.'

The eels slithered around the man's legs. He pushed

himself against the back of the tank. Suddenly the water vibrated and the man shook, his eyes rolling back in his head. For a moment, he went rigid, his hair standing on end, then he slumped into the water, dead.

'A massive electric shock delivered by the fish,' Cryptos said. 'I didn't even have to breed them to make them so large.'

Georgia crushed herself back against the far wall of her tank and stared in horror at the dead man as the eels slithered over him.

Fulton rushed to Georgia's tank and put his hands against it.

'You monster,' Dakkar spat. 'That man was defenceless.'

'You think your precious Oginski's hands are so clean?' Cryptos said, his voice hardening. 'Does your father not execute prisoners?'

'My father would make you pay for the way you've treated me!' Dakkar said coldly.

'Interesting,' Cryptos muttered, stroking his beard. 'You really don't know, do you?'

'Know what?' Dakkar growled back, trying not to stare at the slumped figure in the water.

'Have you heard from your father lately?' Cryptos said, raising his eyebrows.

Dakkar saw Oginski tense. 'No,' he muttered. 'He has many enemies. Oginski has to keep our location secret –'

Cryptos cut Dakkar off with a bellowing laugh. 'Foolish boy!' he said. 'So my brother even has to keep your whereabouts secret from your own father, does he?'

'I don't know,' Dakkar said, casting a searching glance at Oginski.

'You were kidnapped!' Cryptos yelled in triumph. 'Cast your mind back to that day in Liverpool. Were there any formal introductions? Any letters confirming identification?'

'No,' Dakkar said, his chest tightening as he thought back to the day he'd first met Oginski. 'We were being chased. But I knew Count Oginski was going to meet me.'

'My name is Oginski! *I* was going to meet you!' Cryptos barked. 'I sent my men to collect you but my brother beat me to it. Your father never intended him to mentor you – it was me he expected you to meet.'

Dakkar looked from Cryptos to Oginski, who lowered his gaze to the floor.

'I couldn't bear to see you twisted by his philosophy,' Oginski said, his voice barely a whisper. 'When I heard through my contacts that your father was sending you to Cryptos, I knew I had to act.'

'You see, Dakkar, your father wants you to be a strong, single-minded ruler. I've watched you grow up and I spotted your potential many years ago,' Cryptos said. 'I offered to mentor you, to train you in the arts of intrigue and espionage, to become a weapon to liberate not just your own nation but all nations of the world. Your father thought I would train you to become the next Rajah of Bundelkhand but I would make you so much more. I would make you my heir, the next Count Cryptos.'

A thousand questions tore at Dakkar. The last four

years of trusting Oginski, of growing to respect him, flew through his mind. *How could Oginski lie to me like that? Does my father want me to be like Cryptos?* Deep in his heart, Dakkar knew what his father was capable of.

'There's only one question you have to ask yourself, Dakkar,' Oginski said, not meeting his gaze. 'Are you a monster?'

'I disagree,' Cryptos said, meshing his fingers together and resting them under his chin. 'You have to ask yourself about your duty to obey your father. You have to ask yourself how great can you be?' Cryptos clapped his hands and the guards grabbed Dakkar's arms. 'Enough. You will retrieve the Eye of Neptune for me or Georgia Fulton will pay the price. Take them back to their rooms to think on what has been said.'

The guards half carried, half dragged the struggling Dakkar out of the room with Cryptos's parting words ringing in his ears.

'You have a choice to make, Prince of Bundelkhand,' he called after Dakkar. 'Cryptos or Oginski. Duty or deception. Life or death.'

CHAPTER TWENTY-THREE
THE DECISION

Sleep didn't come easily to Dakkar. The lock had been replaced with a bolt on the outside and a guard leaned heavily on the door. Dakkar could hear him shifting position every now and then.

As he lay in his room, Dakkar's stomach felt heavy and his mind wound round and round over the same thoughts, like one of Oginski's clockwork engines. How could Oginski have kidnapped him and tricked him into believing that he was Dakkar's mentor for all those years? Oginski was surely as devious as Cryptos. And was he as ruthless? He remembered the two men who had attacked him in Liverpool. Oginski had dealt with them with singular efficiency.

He remembered his father looking down on him on that last day. 'You are going to learn how to be a leader of men,' his father had said. Dakkar could see his sunken eyes, the long, grey beard barely concealing the pinched cheekbones. 'You will be taught by the best, by a noble-man who has known our hardships.'

His father meant Cryptos. His father wanted him to become a force for destruction, but Oginski had other ideas.

The morning brought Cryptos to Dakkar's door. He stood tall and gaunt, a high, bejewelled collar round his neck.

'Before we embark on this voyage,' he said, rubbing his hands together, 'I've taken Oginski and Fulton off fitting out my *Nautilus* and tasked them with modifying the *Liberty*. As you will be the captain of the craft, I think it's only sensible that you're involved in these developments.'

'Whatever you say,' Dakkar muttered dully. His head ached and he felt tired.

'Just remember that any foolish trickery will result in the death of your friend,' Cryptos said, laying a cold hand on Dakkar's shoulder as they walked out into the corridor. 'Watch my brother. Is he truly any different to me? Would you defy your father to follow him?'

Dakkar shrugged Cryptos's hand away and followed the guards down to the cavern where the *Liberty* lay, dwarfed by the mighty *Nautilus*. Despite his tormented thoughts, Dakkar still marvelled at the huge sub.

The *Liberty* was dangling from a winch above Oginski and Fulton's heads when Dakkar arrived. The two men looked pale and drawn. Clearly neither of them had slept well either.

'Once I have the Eye of Neptune,' Cryptos said, pointing at the *Nautilus*, 'and it is installed in this craft, she will be ready. She will be invincible!'

Cryptos swept away, laughing, leaving Dakkar standing face to face with Oginski.

'Ah, Dakkar,' Oginski said, clearing his throat. 'We need to attach some kind of lifting device to the front of the submersible.'

'We favour pincers of some description, if we can manufacture them,' Fulton added, pushing his spectacles up his nose.

Discussing the practicalities of the modifications to the *Liberty* distracted Dakkar, and for a while he forgot about his dilemma. Cryptos's island fortress proved to be well equipped and Dakkar found himself in a cavernous forge holding strips of glowing red iron with tongs while Oginski hammered them into shape.

'I did think about telling you the truth,' Oginski grunted between hammer blows. 'But I feared your reaction. I couldn't risk you defecting to Cryptos.'

'But why me?' Dakkar asked, shifting the iron to a better position for Oginski to bash.

'Kazmer and I were in India when you were born,' Oginski said, pausing at the anvil for a moment. 'It wasn't long after the Siege of Seringapatam,' he continued, plunging the metal into water and grimacing at the steam that hissed up into his face. 'We'd been supplying the Sultan Tipu with rockets to fight the English but it had come to nought. Your father sheltered us when the English won and Kazmer recognised a kindred spirit in him.'

'My father? Like Cryptos?' Dakkar growled. 'Never.'

'Search your heart, Dakkar,' Oginski said softly, then rammed another strip into the burning hot coals. 'Your father is a brutal man. Like many of us, he has had to fight from the moment he could stand.'

'So Cryptos and my father made a deal?' Dakkar said, getting ready to pluck the iron from the coals.

'When you were old enough, Kazmer was to take you and mould you into a living weapon,' Oginski said, resuming his hammering. He fashioned the iron into a sharp point and held it up as if to illustrate what he was saying. 'Your father had taught you the martial arts of fist, spear and sword. Your time in the English schools hardened your heart against its people. Kazmer was to show you the ways of your enemies. The Europeans.'

'So that I could purge them from my land,' Dakkar finished. 'That doesn't seem a bad thing.'

'But the Brothers Oginski grow old,' the count said. 'They seek new blood as their plots and schemes come to fruition. Having seen you as a child, I couldn't let them corrupt you.'

Dakkar fell silent, mulling over what Oginski had said.

The day wore on and the work became fatiguing. Dakkar worried about Georgia. He watched Robert Fulton as the man sweated and struggled to assemble the metal arms. A team of Qualar lent their strength to the work but Dakkar could see that Fulton fretted too.

A leaden weight lay somewhere in Dakkar's stomach. He'd found Oginski, only to discover deception. Dakkar couldn't meet Oginski's eye.

'You could have told me,' he said to Oginski. 'You didn't have to keep all this from me.'

'You were ten years old, Dakkar,' Oginski replied. 'You ran away so many times anyway. Would you really have understood if I had told you that I was guiding you down a more peaceful path?'

'Probably not, and perhaps for good reason. Look where it's got us!' Dakkar snorted. 'I thought about this last night and it seems to me that the only way to beat Cryptos is to be like Cryptos . . .'

Day and night were hard to distinguish in this underground world but sore muscles and heavy eyelids told Dakkar that he had worked a full, hard day. His head ached with thinking but he had come to a decision when Cryptos appeared to appraise the work.

'Things always look worse before they improve,' he said with a thin smile, tilting his head.

The *Liberty* looked a mess. Oginski had drilled holes in the bow of the craft to allow the arms to be controlled from within.

'I've made a decision,' Dakkar said.

Oginski and Fulton froze.

Cryptos raised one thin eyebrow. 'Have you now?' he murmured.

'I will join you,' Dakkar said.

'Dakkar, no!' Oginski gasped. 'Think about what you're saying!'

'It's no good,' Dakkar said. 'My mind is made up. Count Cryptos, I will become your apprentice.'

CHAPTER TWENTY-FOUR
THE MOLE

'Dakkar, you don't know what you're doing!' Oginski said, his face pale and serious.

'I know exactly what I'm doing,' Dakkar spat. 'You tricked me. You tried to change me and you would have turned me against my own father if you'd had your way.'

Cryptos remained silent, standing with his hands crossed, like a vicar awaiting his flock at the church door.

'I only did what I did to save you from the evil and destruction that this man peddles,' Oginski pleaded.

'You deceived me,' Dakkar said. 'I realise now that my true path is with Cryptos.'

Oginski glared at Dakkar in disbelief.

'You have chosen well,' Cryptos said, clapping his hands together.

Dakkar gritted his teeth as Cryptos put a bony arm round his shoulder.

'Dakkar, don't do this!' Oginski cried, leaping forward. Qualar guards grabbed him and pulled him back. 'Don't become a monster.'

'Come, you must rest, and then tomorrow I shall show you such wonders!' Cryptos said, and ushered Dakkar from the cavern.

'Dakkar! Come back!' Oginski called after him.

Dakkar closed his eyes and allowed himself to be led away.

When he reached his room, which was no longer locked, Dakkar lay in bed staring at the ceiling. He could still hear Oginski's pleas, but this was the only way. If he could persuade Cryptos that he really had decided to be his apprentice, then he had a greater chance of defeating him. It meant deceiving Oginski, however. Dakkar sighed and, slowly, sleep took him.

Whether it was exhaustion, Dakkar didn't know, but he awoke the following morning having slept like the dead. He opened his eyes a crack and jumped up, realising that he was not alone.

A Qualar stood to attention at the foot of the bed. He wore breeches and a shirt of green silk. His milky eyes stared ahead. Only his gills moved, opening and closing in the side of his neck.

'Forgive the intrusion, your highness,' he said in a gasping voice. 'But I was sent by Count Cryptos to act as your manservant.'

'Excellent,' Dakkar said, bemused by the sight of the strange fish-man. 'And what shall I call you?'

'My name is Olszar,' the fish-man said, holding his chin up, 'Shoal Lord of Qualarium.'

'You're a king?' Dakkar said, staring at the Qualar.

The fish-man's head fell. 'Once I was,' he said. 'Now I serve Cryptos and . . . and you.'

Olszar isn't happy with Cryptos – that's clear, Dakkar thought, pursing his lips. 'Have you eaten?'

Olszar shook his head. 'I was directed by Cryptos to bring your food first,' he said, waving a hand over a platter of fruit, baked fish and bread. 'And these clothes.' He pointed to a fine suit of black linen that lay across the foot of the bed.

'Then sit, Olszar,' Dakkar said, pulling up a chair. 'And, once I'm dressed, you can tell me how Count Cryptos came to rule your world.'

'I'm not permitted to be too familiar with you,' Olszar said, watching Dakkar's face intently.

'I won't tell Cryptos,' Dakkar said, dragging the shirt and suit on. It was fine material, light and cool in the stuffy underground environment. He sat at the table and gestured for Olszar to join him.

'I'm not sure it is wise,' Olszar muttered, bowing.

'You can trust me,' Dakkar said, holding Olszar's gaze.

Olszar gave a short nod and joined him at the table. 'It's a sad tale. The Qualar are a mighty race,' Olszar said, settling on the chair and glancing at the door. 'From the blue city of Qualarium, the Qualar hunt across the ocean bed. We take the harvest we need from the sea. We keep away from the eyes of men.'

'But what happened?' Dakkar asked, offering him the fish. 'How did Cryptos find you?'

'We found him,' Olszar said with a shake of his scaly head. 'His ship sank in battle. A Qualar hunter found him and saved him from drowning. At first he charmed us, taking in the wonders of our world with bewildered amazement. Then he began to question our warriors and hunters. Why hadn't they taken the land world too? Why did we hide away?'

'And why do you hide away?' Dakkar said, chewing thoughtfully on some fruit.

'Forgive me,' Olszar said, something close to a grin crossing his face, 'but humans are mad. They kill and torture each other. They are full of pointless suffering.'

Dakkar nodded. 'You may be right.'

'Cryptos whispered words of greed and evil in our ears. He divided us,' Olszar said. His face dropped. 'He found our spawning chambers where we store and protect our unhatched young. He threatened to destroy them.'

'If there are so many Qualar, can't you rise up?' Dakkar said. 'Can't you overthrow Cryptos?'

'A shoal divided cannot escape the shark,' Olszar sighed, his gills fanning the air. 'As long as there are Qualar who carry spears for him and as long as he can destroy our spawning chambers, we are lost. Those who side with Cryptos bring him creatures from the deepest regions of the sea. He breeds and grows them to gigantic proportions. They shepherd and control them for him. Such were the creatures that attacked you.'

'Cryptos has bred land animals too,' Dakkar said. 'I saw a huge ape.'

'He made those himself,' Olszar replied.

Dakkar sat in silence for a moment, chewing a crust of bread.

'I should not be talking of this,' Olszar said, his voice laden with worry. 'You have chosen to be this man's apprentice.'

'I have,' Dakkar said, nodding. 'But you have nothing to fear from me.'

Olszar furrowed his scaly brow in confusion and was about to speak, when the door flew open.

Cryptos stood, eyeing the seated pair. Three human guards stood behind him carrying rifles.

'My prince,' he said with a tight smile, 'one shouldn't be overfamiliar with the servants. They might get ideas above their station.'

'I was just learning about the history of the Qualar,' Dakkar said, holding Cryptos's gaze. 'I see nothing wrong in that. A good ruler understands his subjects.'

'Noble sentiments, Dakkar,' Cryptos said. 'But their fear is all that is required for now. Olszar, leave us.'

'No, I would have him stay,' Dakkar said, leaping to his feet. 'He's my servant after all.'

A scowl flashed across Cryptos's face. 'You are quite the petulant one,' he said, regaining his composure.

'I learn quickly,' Dakkar said, putting his hands on his hips. 'You said I should be single-minded. Well, I am.'

For a moment, Cryptos stared warily at Dakkar and then he laughed. 'Very well,' he said, clapping his hands. 'Olszar can join us.' But his face hardened as he spoke to the Qualar. 'Just remember you are no longer Shoal Lord.'

Olszar lowered his head.

Cryptos led them out of the room and along the corridor into which Dakkar had first crept.

'This island has been my fortress for some time now,' Cryptos said, tracing his finger along the wall. 'It's a warren of tunnels.'

'It's a wonder the whole thing doesn't collapse,' Dakkar muttered, peering down one of the many side tunnels as they passed.

'You're right to wonder.' Cryptos smiled. 'I suspended excavations after a few unfortunate cave-ins.'

They stopped at a huge door. The guards pushed it open and Cryptos began to step through but Olszar hung back.

'Please,' he croaked, bowing his head even lower. 'Don't make me go in here. I cannot bear to see my people suffering in this way.'

Dakkar looked past Cryptos to see the chamber with the huge machine. Hundreds of Qualar laboured and suffered in there. He swallowed hard as he looked at Olszar's tortured face.

'Enough,' Cryptos snapped. 'They are no longer your people, Olszar. Don't forget that. Now follow.'

From up above, Dakkar hadn't fully appreciated the hardships of the chamber. Now, up close, it looked like a scene from Dante's *Inferno*. Men, grimy and stripped to the waist, mingled with Qualar, all gasping and panting as they smashed at the glassy rock with picks and hammers. Others dragged plates of steel across the ground to the scaffold that enmeshed the colossal machine. Steam boiled from the cracks in the rock wall, making men and Qualar alike curse and spit. High above, the circle of the main vent tormented them with a glimpse of far-off daylight.

'I think you've already met the taskmaster,' Cryptos said, pointing to the centre of the crush. 'This is my right-hand man, Mr Phoebus Blight.'

Dakkar stifled a gasp, recognising the familiar hunched figure who shuffled along the lines of staggering men, lashing out at any slackers with a riding crop.

'The m-man at the village,' Dakkar stammered, then he glared at Cryptos. 'He was with you at the castle.'

Phoebus Blight raised his tricorne hat at Dakkar and gave a mocking welcome bow and a crooked grin. Then he fell to beating the unfortunate slaves again.

'He doesn't talk much,' Cryptos said, picking some dirt from under his long fingernails. 'Not since I had his tongue ripped out. His loyalty seems to grow the more I mistreat him.'

'Another monster,' Dakkar murmured.

'You want revenge on him, don't you, and on me?' Cryptos grinned.

'Yes,' Dakkar said, staring Cryptos in the eye. 'But I can wait until you've taught me everything you know.'

'Excellent.' Cryptos laughed. 'I would have been suspicious of you if you'd said no. There's honesty in hatred. Kindle that in your heart. That is what will give you power.'

Dakkar forced a mirthless grin and cast his eyes over the huge machine.

'It's a drill, Dakkar. I call it the Mole,' Cryptos yelled above the noise of the working slaves. 'A massive digging machine. Powered by the Eye of Neptune, the point will burrow deep into the earth's core, bringing lava to the surface.'

'And what good will that do?' Dakkar shouted back.

'Observe.' Cryptos pointed to the deep tunnels at the side of the room and the slaves staggering into them with barrels. 'These men are packing the vents of the volcano with gunpowder. Only a few feet of rock stand between us and the mighty ocean. Once my Mole machine begins digging, they will blast open the vents, allowing millions of tons of seawater to pour into the chamber.'

Dakkar still looked perplexed.

'When the cold water of the sea meets the inferno from below, there will be a catastrophic explosion the like of which has never been seen,' Cryptos screamed. His eyes blazed and spittle flew from his lips. 'The sea will rise up and flood every coast on the Atlantic. Earthquakes will shake the coastline of an entire continent. Thousands of tons of ash will be pumped into the air, blotting out the sun. In short, there will be chaos.'

'No sun, no crops,' Dakkar said, staring at the Mole. 'Famine across the globe. Devastation along the coast of America. Every seaport, every naval base destroyed.'

'And I will be safe below the surface of the sea in the *Nautilus* submersible, with my army of giant sea monsters,' Cryptos said, gripping Dakkar's arm with a shaking hand. 'Poised to strike at whatever shipyard remains unscathed.'

'The beginning of the end,' Dakkar finished. For a moment he felt numb. It all sounded unreal but he knew thousands of people would die. The world would be turned upside down.

'The beginning of a new age,' Cryptos corrected, clapping his hands. 'One that, ultimately, you will inherit.'

CHAPTER TWENTY-FIVE
THE TEST

Since Dakkar had declared his allegiance to Cryptos, Oginski proved sullen and uncommunicative as they worked on the *Liberty*. Two days had passed and they fitted her out in virtual silence. Sometimes Cryptos stood and watched them with narrow eyes as if searching for some evidence of a plot.

A guard still followed them wherever they went, shadowing them. Olszar waited on Dakkar too.

Despite this, Dakkar found he was free to wander the labyrinth of tunnels. If he came close to a door that concealed something sensitive, his guard would grunt and slam his spear butt on the ground.

'We are forbidden to enter, my prince,' Olszar would say.

One door was painted red. Dakkar noticed copper lining the base of the door and the floor.

'Explosives?' he whispered to Olszar, who nodded.

'How did you know?' the servant whispered back.

'The copper. It reduces the chance of men's boots striking a spark,' Dakkar murmured. The guard banged his spear to the floor and they moved on but Dakkar made a mental note of where the door was.

Another slave hurried to meet them and said something in the strange gurgling language of the Qualar.

'It seems Cryptos wants you in the throne room,' Olszar interpreted as they hurried up the steps.

Cryptos sat in his chair as Dakkar entered. Georgia was slumped in the corner of the tank just as she had been when he'd last seen her. She jumped up when he came in and pressed her hands to the front of the glass box.

'My guards tell me that you've been exploring the complex,' Cryptos said, leaning forward in his chair.

'Don't you trust me?' Dakkar countered.

'Should I?' Cryptos replied, sitting back in his seat.

'Probably not, if you want me to be ruthless,' Dakkar said. 'I haven't forgiven you any more than I've forgiven Oginski. I will have my revenge on both of you.'

'Dakkar?' Georgia said, the glass muffling her voice. 'What's going on? Where is everyone?'

Dakkar looked at her tear-stained face and gritted his teeth, forcing down the stab of regret.

'I'd be disappointed if you didn't want my head,' Cryptos said, leering at him. 'But I need some kind of assertion of loyalty to our cause.' He stood up and walked over to Georgia, who spat at the glass in his direction.

The eels squirmed and wriggled in their slimy tank next to hers.

'Kill her,' Cryptos snapped, stepping back to allow Dakkar access to the lever that would release the eels.

Dakkar bit his tongue and felt the blood drain from his face. Georgia's eyes widened and she slammed her fists against the side of the tank.

'Prove to me that you are committed to the cause of Count Cryptos,' he hissed. 'Pull the lever. Kill her.'

'Very well,' Dakkar said, swallowing hard. His throat felt dry as he walked over to the lever. He reached out to grasp it.

'What are you doing?' Georgia yelled.

His sweating fingers closed around the ivory handle.

'Dakkar, have you gone mad? It's me, Georgia!'

'Don't you ever shut up?' Dakkar snapped, and tensed his arm muscles as if to slam the lever down.

'Stop!' Cryptos barked. His face split into a broad grin.

Dakkar dropped his hand. For a moment, Georgia's breathless sobs were the only noise in the room.

'Why did you stop me?' Dakkar frowned, doing his best to look frustrated.

'We need her a little longer,' Cryptos said. 'Fulton and Oginski would down tools if they knew she was dead already. The *Liberty* will be ready tomorrow. Oginski will show you how to control the pincers and then we will take the Eye of Neptune.'

'Can I go now?' Dakkar murmured. He felt cold inside.

Georgia had recovered her breath and stood glaring at Dakkar.

'Just you wait, mister!' she bellowed. 'When I get out of here, you'll be so sorry.'

Dakkar didn't look at her as he stalked out of the room.

On the evening of the next day, Cryptos summoned Dakkar to the cave to be familiarised with the controls. Dakkar hurried down, followed by Olszar and the guard. They gasped and gulped as they tried to keep up with him.

'You race to the cavern,' Olszar grunted, catching up with him. 'In the water we would beat you, but on land we are slow!'

Dakkar glanced back at the struggling guard. 'If you can,' he whispered to Olszar, 'give me a few seconds alone with Oginski. I need to talk to him.'

Olszar frowned but nodded and slowed down as the guard caught up.

Cryptos paced the jetty, rubbing his hands. Oginski and Fulton stood, flanked by guards, their arms hanging limply at their sides. Oginski looked defeated.

Behind the *Nautilus*, like a duckling with its mother, the *Liberty* bobbed on the illuminated water. She was tilted forward slightly by the weight of the hurriedly built arms that poked in front of the craft.

'At last,' Cryptos snapped. 'Once I have the Eye of Neptune, the Mole will be complete.'

'And not just the Mole, Count Cryptos,' said Dakkar.

'You said the Eye could be used to power a whole fleet of submersibles and, I imagine, all manner of other terrible machines.'

'If my research is correct,' Cryptos said, his eyes gleaming, 'then the Eye of Neptune is a Voltalith, a meteor that carries a massive electrical charge. Only a mere fragment will be needed to turn the giant auger.'

'Then what are we waiting for?' Dakkar clambered on to the *Liberty*. 'Oginski will show me how to operate the pincers.'

Dakkar gave Olszar a meaningful glance and clambered down into the *Liberty*. Dakkar's guard and Oginski followed. It felt good to be back in the familiar surroundings and, for a second, Dakkar almost forgot the rift between them. Dakkar removed his black linen jacket and laid it on the cases that held the Sea Arrows. Oginski showed Dakkar the levers that opened and closed the pincers and the lock that screwed shut once the object had been picked up.

Dakkar's guard stood over them watching every move. Olszar appeared, climbing down the ladder.

'Did I ask you down here?' Dakkar said, raising his eyebrows at Olszar.

'No, but . . .' Olszar began, looking deep into Dakkar's eyes. Dakkar gave a slight nod.

'Don't answer me back!' Dakkar snapped. 'Get out now!'

Olszar gave a roar and clamped his hands round Dakkar's throat. Immediately the guard lunged forward and ended up grappling with Olszar, blocking the hatch and stopping the others from climbing down. Dakkar staggered away from the wrestling pair.

'Is that your toolbox?' he hissed, nodding at the long rectangular box at Oginski's feet.

Oginski nodded and then his eyes widened as Dakkar whipped open the lid to the Sea Arrows and pulled one out. He dropped it into the toolbox and flicked the lid shut.

Grabbing a large spanner, he swung it down on Olszar's head. The Qualar crumpled to the floor, leaving the panting guard to struggle to his feet.

'What is going on in here?' Cryptos shouted, as he climbed down into the lower cabin.

'Olszar attacked me,' Dakkar said. 'But I knocked him out.'

'He shall pay with his life,' Cryptos hissed.

'No,' Dakkar said, kicking the unconscious Qualar. 'Make him work. Make him a slave like the rest of his people. Such a humiliation would be worse than death to him.'

'You're learning fast,' Cryptos said with a snigger. 'Take him to the slave pit and throw him in!'

Dakkar gave Oginski a fleeting grin and watched the crumpled, defeated look vanish.

'Cryptos, look out!' Dakkar yelled. 'He has an explosive in that box!'

Oginski stared in disbelief as the guard stamped forward and whipped the butt end of his spear at him. The wood made a hollow clunk as it struck Oginski's temple, sending him tumbling to the ground.

Dakkar snatched the Sea Arrow from the box and held it up for Cryptos to see.

'Well done, my apprentice!' he enthused. 'If I doubted you before, I no longer do.'

'Dakkar . . . you betrayed me . . .' Oginski stammered as two guards dragged him to his feet.

'Now you know how it feels,' Dakkar said, gritting his teeth.

'Lock him away,' Cryptos said, stroking his chin. 'Secure the submersible and prepare supplies. Tomorrow we seek the Eye of Neptune.'

Dakkar grinned and picked up his linen jacket, hugging it to him.

'You like the trappings of wealth and power, I see,' Cryptos said, nodding at Dakkar's fine jacket.

'Oh yes,' Dakkar murmured, and clambered out of the *Liberty*, still clutching it. He hugged the second Sea Arrow, wrapped in the fine cloth, to his chest like a baby.

CHAPTER TWENTY-SIX
THE EYE

Dakkar stood poring over the sea chart. The contour lines snaked and swirled in front of him in a confusing mass. Here and there rock escarpments and coral reefs jutted out, deep chasms that scored the seabed.

'Although the Qualar fear this area, they could describe it to a degree,' Cryptos said, tracing a long, black fingernail across the paper. 'The chart I had drawn from their descriptions may be unreliable but it's the best we can do. The volcano vents out here and apparently smoke boils from the seabed. The Eye of Neptune can't be missed.'

'The seabed looks treacherous,' Dakkar murmured, craning his neck to look at the chart.

'Two days from now, my plan will be complete,' Cryptos said to himself, stroking his straggly beard. 'Two days . . .'

'I'll need the Fulton girl,' Dakkar said, cutting over him.

'What?' Cryptos said, scowling. Dakkar could see a vein pulsing at his temple. 'What on earth for?'

'She's as good a captain as me,' Dakkar said reasonably. 'She'll be able to hold the *Liberty* steady while I grab the Eye with the pincers. I can't do it on my own.'

'But Phoebus can do that,' Cryptos said, clenching his fists.

'Can he describe what he can see as he captains the ship?' Dakkar said with a dismissive gesture. 'Has he sailed her across the ocean?'

'No, but he is reliable,' Cryptos said.

'Don't you trust me?' Dakkar asked, raising an eyebrow. 'I saved you from Oginski's bomb. I've shown you that I'll happily take the girl's life if she causes trouble.'

Cryptos narrowed his eyes. His mouth became a thin line. 'Very well,' he said. 'But Phoebus Blight goes with you too. That girl is too handy with her fists.'

Dakkar hadn't expected Georgia to be quite so handy with her fists.

'How could you betray us like that?' she hissed, bounding at him and pinning him to the ground. 'You . . .' she punctuated each phrase with a blow, ' . . . would . . .' stars flashed in Dakkar's eyes, '. . . have . . .' his head banged against the decking of the jetty, '. . . killed me!'

Grabbing her shoulders, Dakkar rolled and tried to free himself. The iron taste of blood filled his mouth and his head echoed with the painful thump he'd just received. The guards managed to drag her off him.

'And you want to take this wildcat with you?' Cryptos laughed. 'I did warn you.'

'She'll calm down,' Dakkar said, staggering to his feet and wiping his mouth with the back of his hand.

'We trusted you, Dakkar,' Georgia yelled, lunging at him again. 'And you let us down!'

'It was the only way,' Dakkar said, spitting blood into the water. 'Now, are you going to help me get the Eye of Neptune or do you want to go back to your eel tank?'

'I think I prefer the eels to you,' Georgia snarled.

'Enough of this prattle,' Cryptos cut in. 'I'm impatient to have the Eye of Neptune in my grasp. If Miss Fulton will not cooperate, then you'll have to take your chances with just my man.'

Phoebus Blight shuffled forward and stared at Dakkar.

'I need you to come with me,' Dakkar said to Georgia in a low voice, his eyes pleading.

Georgia frowned. 'All right then,' she said slowly. 'But don't think I've forgotten.'

They climbed into the *Liberty* followed by Blight, who made eager grunting noises, running his hands over the controls and the brass rails.

'One day, my friend,' Cryptos said, staring down at him from the hatch above, 'you will have a whole fleet of these to command.'

'Nnngh!' Blight lifted his scarred face to Cryptos and gave a twisted grin.

Dakkar and Georgia climbed down into the lower

cabin while Blight sat in the captain's seat above, admiring the controls.

'My Qualar will escort you as far as they dare,' Cryptos called down. 'After that you're on your own. Do not fail me.'

The hatch slammed shut and Dakkar heard the ropes being cast off. Georgia climbed up, grimacing at Blight, who shuffled out of the captain's seat with a grunt of displeasure. He planted himself next to her, watching every move closely.

They began to move and Dakkar felt calmed by the whirr of the engines. Outside, the shadowy forms of the Qualar flitted among the glowing jellyfish. Soon they crossed the cave threshold and Dakkar remembered the moment when they had arrived. So much had changed in only a few days.

Dakkar tried hard to catch Georgia's eye to communicate to her that she could trust him, but Blight glared at them both.

'We basically follow the seabed down,' Georgia said, lifting the chart up and squinting at it. 'If you imagine the island to be the peak of an underwater mountain, then we're just travelling down the side of it.'

'Let Blight steer for a while and help me check that the pincers work,' Dakkar said.

Blight gave a grunt and frowned.

'Don't you want to captain the sub?' Dakkar said, looking surprised. 'Your master trusts me and so should you.'

Blight was torn, Dakkar could tell. The man's piggy

eyes flitted from Dakkar to Georgia and the wheel. He licked his slug-like lips and then gave one curt nod.

Georgia swapped places and followed Dakkar down to the lower cabin.

'Don't say a word,' Dakkar whispered. 'Just listen and answer my questions. If the captain's cabin floods, what happens?'

'I don't know. The ship might capsize.' Georgia frowned. 'Why? What are you . . . ?'

Dakkar put a finger to his lips. 'Trust me. Can it be pumped clear of water?'

'No, but if the top hatch were shut the water in the top cabin could flow into the bottom, making it –' Georgia began.

'Right, listen,' Dakkar said in a low voice. 'Once we've got the Eye of Neptune and we're in shallower water, I want you to open the hatch and flood the captain's cabin.'

'What?' Georgia stared at Dakkar in disbelief.

'If Blight and I are in the lower cabin, we'll have to shut the hatch and seal ourselves in or risk sinking the sub,' Dakkar said. 'You'll have the chance to swim free. I'll smuggle a Sea Arrow into the top cabin. You escape with it and make your way to the top of the volcano crater.'

'But I thought –' Georgia began.

'I know you thought I had joined Cryptos, but I haven't. Now listen,' Dakkar continued. 'In two days' time, I'm going to try and get the Qualar slaves to revolt. I need you up above to drop the arrow on to the huge machine that sits in the middle of the volcano. You can't miss.'

'But the sea will be crawling with Cryptos's Qualar guards,' Georgia said. 'What if I get caught?'

'Cryptos will never let us free,' Dakkar said, shaking his head. 'Do you want to take this chance or go back to the eel tank?'

Georgia looked pale. 'You're a strange one, Prince Dakkar,' she said, putting a hand on his shoulder. 'I'm sorry I doubted you.'

'Will you do it?' Dakkar asked.

'Nnngh!' Blight shouted from above. Clearly there had been too much whispering.

Georgia nodded her head and Dakkar gave her a genuine grin.

Georgia scrambled back up into the captain's seat, leaving Dakkar to stare out at the shoal of Qualar that escorted them. The seabed sloped downward; coral and seaweed swept past seemingly at angles with the sub.

They sank deeper and the Qualar began to fall back. Soon the water darkened and the planks of the *Liberty* creaked ominously as the water pressure increased.

Dakkar felt as though he had something blocking his ears and his head ached. He lit oil lamps and placed them at the viewing portholes down below.

The seaweed thinned out, revealing skeletal coral stalks that looked like dead hands reaching for the distant surface. Strange, luminous fish glared at them through the portholes, all teeth and eyes.

Up in the captain's cabin, Blight dabbed his brow with a handkerchief and Georgia peered ahead as she negotiated rocky outcrops and thick branches of coral. A tense hush descended on the *Liberty*.

In the distance, a blue light began to glimmer. Dakkar and Georgia stared in wonder as shoals of the glowing fish swarmed around their boat, lighting up the side of the volcano.

Up ahead, something else added to the blue glow.

A vent poked out of the side of the volcano, spewing boiling black gas up into the sea. Around it lay hundreds of colossal, wide-open, white clams. Each was the size of the *Liberty*, at least, and they dotted the seabed as far as Dakkar could see.

The largest sat at the very base of the vent with what looked like an electric blue pearl snapping and fizzing at its heart. Arcs of electric blue charge leapt and curled around it like whips of lightning. The light bounced off huge pearls in the other shells, dazzling Dakkar and making him shield his eyes with his hand.

'The Eye of Neptune,' Dakkar said. 'It's beautiful.'

'It's deadly,' Georgia replied, slowing the *Liberty* right down. 'How are we going to pick it up?'

'The pincers are coated with rubber from the Americas,' Dakkar said. 'Apparently it neutralises the electric charge.'

'Nngh!' Blight grunted, pointing at the Voltalith.

'I think he wants us to get on with it,' Georgia said, curling her lip at Blight.

They drifted towards the glowing shell. Dakkar hurried down to the lower cabin to prepare the grippers. The

alien world of the seabed looked even stranger cast in the
blue light. He grimaced. They were over the outer clam
shells now and he could see bones scattered around them,
some complete, some fragmented. The water outside was
deadly.

Perhaps the clams live off the dead remains, he thought,
shivering at the thought of the molluscs filtering the
rotten slivers of flesh through their bodies.

The light became more intense as they drew nearer to
the Eye. The downy hair on Dakkar's arm stood up and he
felt his scalp prickle.

Georgia had killed the engine and they drifted gently.
Dakkar watched through the front porthole as the two
pincers glided either side of the Voltalith. Dakkar staggered slightly as they stopped with a bump. For a second,
he stared at the intense blue light that crackled and fizzed
around them, mesmerised.

Shaking himself, Dakkar jumped forward and gripped
the inside handles of the pincers and shut them. His
fingers tingled as the arms closed round the blue rock.
The well-oiled joints slid and clicked into place, and
Dakkar turned the screw that locked them.

'Take it away,' Dakkar called up.

The engines whirred but a sudden lurch sent Dakkar
stumbling to the stern of the cabin. A metallic thump
vibrated through the front of the *Liberty* and Dakkar
watched in horror as a clam closed round the pincers,
shrouding the light of the Eye of Neptune.

'We're held fast,' Georgia yelled.

Blight clambered down and squinted through the porthole at the bone-white teeth of the shell that had clamped the arms tight.

'Give it full power,' Dakkar said, looking over Blight's shoulder.

The whole sub shuddered as Georgia tried to back away from the clam. The engines whined and clanked but nothing happened.

'Ack!' Blight shouted, waving his arms at Dakkar in frustration.

Georgia pushed the *Liberty* forward and then rammed her into reverse, sending Blight and Dakkar tumbling across the floor of the cabin.

'It's no good,' Georgia gasped. 'We're trapped.'

CHAPTER TWENTY-SEVEN
DEATH GRIP

The *Liberty*'s engine clunked and grumbled as Dakkar and Blight wound it to full power. Georgia reversed again, twisting the wheel to make the sub jag from side to side. The planks of the *Liberty* groaned.

'Stop!' Dakkar cried.

Water had dribbled from the prow, where a combination of rubberised leather and oiled cloth waterproofed the holes that allowed the pincers to move and be controlled from inside the ship.

The air had become stale and the crew's breathing shallow. Sweat trickled down Dakkar's temples. The stink of Phoebus Blight filled his nostrils as the man stood next to him.

'We could let the Eye go and see if it releases us,' Dakkar panted.

'Could we blast it with the last Sea Arrow?' Georgia asked.

'We'd blow ourselves up,' Dakkar murmured.

'Nah!' Blight growled, shaking his head. He tapped the side of his nose and lowered his hands up and down in a calming motion.

'You think if we keep still the clam will open again?' Dakkar said, pouting his lip.

Blight nodded enthusiastically. 'An pah!' he yelled, skidding his fist across the palm of his other, open hand.

'Then we back out quickly?' Georgia interpreted.

'But how long do we wait?' Dakkar wondered aloud.

He sat down on the floor of the *Liberty* and stared out of the porthole. *If I just set the last Sea Arrow off here and now, the Eye might be destroyed and Cryptos would be foiled,* Dakkar thought. *Maybe Oginski can find some way to escape and defeat his brother on his own.*

He shook his head. *No, I can't sacrifice Georgia too. I have to get out of this and stop Cryptos myself.*

The heat grew stifling. Dakkar felt dizzy with the pressure. His head ached and he was losing track of time.

'Aah!' Blight whispered, bringing Dakkar to.

The clam's shells were beginning to part. It was opening. The blue light of the Eye of Neptune crackled to life once more.

'Georgia, can you see?' Dakkar hissed up to her.

'I can,' she said quietly.

'Wait for it to open fully,' Dakkar said, watching the shell edge lift. 'Wait, wait, wait . . . Now!'

Georgia rammed the *Liberty* into reverse. Bubbles frothed around the portholes and the engine whined and clunked. Dakkar was thrown on to the floor as they were catapulted back. They were free!

The Eye of Neptune hung before them in the grip of the pincers, lighting the way as they turned and began to climb back to the surface.

Blight sat staring at the Voltalith from the cabin below while Georgia steered them over the sloping seabed. Dakkar glanced at the Sea Arrow box. It was behind Blight and out of his line of vision. Dakkar eased over to the box and lifted the lid. It creaked horribly and he froze. Blight seemed engrossed in the flickering deadliness of the Eye. Lifting the explosive out of the box, Dakkar slid across the lower cabin and crept up the steps.

He placed the missile to the side of Georgia's seat.

'When we get to a depth you can handle,' Dakkar whispered, 'shut the bottom hatch and swim out with the arrow.'

'But I can't get out with water pouring in!' A thin sheen of sweat covered Georgia's brow. 'I'll have to wait for the water to fill this cabin before I can get out, and that may capsize the sub.'

'Don't worry, I'll handle that,' Dakkar said in a low voice.

'And what about the Qualar?' she said, her knuckles white on the wheel.

'I don't think they'll come near the Eye of Neptune,' Dakkar reassured her. 'Just don't swim near it yourself! Good luck.'

Dakkar climbed back down and glanced at Blight but

he still sat hypnotised by the electric storm flickering in front of him.

The water grew lighter and Dakkar felt a little less thickheaded as they came nearer the surface. His palms felt slick and he couldn't stop glancing up at the hatch to the captain's cabin. *When will Georgia make her move?*

Blight was preoccupied, watching the death throes of fish that swam too close to the Eye of Neptune. He grinned as they writhed and twisted in agony. He turned and pointed at a small squid that floated by, its legs rigid. Then his eyes widened.

Dakkar turned just as the hatch slammed shut. He dived over in a feigned attempt to grab the handle to the hatch and ended up tripping Blight, sending them both into a heap on the floor.

'Rarrgh!' Blight yelled, clambering up the ladder and grabbing the hatch handle.

'No!' Dakkar cried, pulling him back down to the floor again. 'Listen. She's opened the outer hatch. You'll flood the sub.'

Blight looked on in horror as the sound of water hammering on the hatch door subsided. The upper cabin was full. Dakkar listened and was rewarded by a second thud as Georgia closed the outer door. Now the *Liberty* listed as the weight of the water above them began to drag the sub upside down.

Dakkar scrambled for the inside door before they were completely capsized and dragged the handle open. Blight gave a bellow of rage as gallons of seawater roared in from above, soaking them both and sending the *Liberty* rolling upright again. They tumbled from one side of the sub to the next, bumping and banging into things. A chair clipped Blight in the temple and the table slammed into Dakkar, knocking the wind out of him. He crawled across the wet floor, dodging cases and tubes of sea charts as they clattered around. On the third or fourth roll of the boat, Dakkar lunged forward and heaved himself into the captain's cabin. He settled the ship but there was no sign of Georgia or the Sea Arrow.

Blight climbed up, trailing a waterfall from his sodden clothes. He slumped beside Dakkar, glowering through the porthole as if he might see Georgia waving to him as she swam past. He slammed his fist on the wheel of the *Liberty* and yelled some incoherent curse.

'She won't get far,' Dakkar said to Blight. 'Those Qualar will find her – that's if she doesn't drown.'

Blight gave a nasty smile that told Dakkar he hoped for the latter.

They returned to the cavern in silence, Dakkar hardly noticing the beauty of the jellyfish and the distant shapes of the wary Qualar.

Cryptos dismissed with a shrug the news that Georgia had escaped. He stood leering at the Eye of Neptune as it sat sizzling in the water at the front of the *Liberty*.

'Excellent,' he murmured. 'You have both done well.' He clapped his hands and four human guards dashed forward. 'Place the Voltalith into the rubberised sling and bring it to my laboratory. Be careful not to touch it or you will die in an instant. I'd hate for it to be dropped.'

'Nagh,' Blight growled, and pointed to the water.

Cryptos turned to face him. 'The girl doesn't matter. If she survived, my God, we'll soon recapture her.'

I hope not, thought Dakkar, following them out of the cavern.

'Success is so close!' Cryptos said. 'I will slice this Voltalith into sections. Each one will power a different device, including the Mole. It's best not to tell Oginski and Fulton about the girl. They're modifying the *Nautilus*'s engine to accept the Eye of Neptune and I don't want them becoming difficult. Soon it will begin.'

Dakkar forced a smile, then went to his room to change and to put the next part of his plan into action.

A few hours later, Dakkar crept from his room down the corridor. He'd noticed a lot of activity. Guards were carrying boxes and sacks. It seemed they were packing up. Dakkar moved among the bustle unnoticed. His bodyguard had disappeared and Dakkar wondered whether this was because Cryptos trusted him now or because everyone was needed to clear the island.

When it goes up, anyone left behind will be killed in an instant, Dakkar thought as he squeezed past people.

He came to the slave chamber and pushed the door open. A Qualar guard blocked his path with a spear.

'Do you not know who I am?' Dakkar spat, glaring up

at the guard. 'I am Count Cryptos's heir apparent. Would you make an enemy of me so soon?'

The guard glanced around for some higher authority but Blight was clearly still recovering from his undersea ordeal and wasn't present. Finally the guard pulled back his spear and Dakkar strode through, searching the chamber for Olszar.

He found the Shoal Lord sitting with a group of other Qualar at the side of the cave. Human guards stood close by, rifles clutched in their hands.

'We have a few minutes' rest,' Olszar murmured, looking sidelong at the nearest guard, 'before we resume. The work is nearly complete though. And there are fewer guards.'

Dakkar laid his jacket down next to Olszar.

'This island is going to be blown apart,' Dakkar said quietly. 'In a few days' time you and your loyal followers will be dead. I want to prevent that.'

'If we fail, then Cryptos will destroy our spawning chambers,' Olszar replied, lowering his head. 'He will doom our race.'

'But if we succeed,' Dakkar said, 'then you will be free and the Qualar can live as one again.'

'What is your plan?' Olszar muttered as the guard wandered out of earshot.

'In two days,' Dakkar said under his breath, 'my friend Georgia will drop an explosive from up there.' He glanced up at the hole high in the darkness. 'Under my jacket is another charge. Can you attach it to the Mole?'

'We can try,' Olszar whispered back. 'It was worth a bump on the head then?' He smiled slightly and rubbed his head.

'Well worth it,' Dakkar said. 'Are you with me?'

'We won't sit here and wait to die,' Olszar hissed, narrowing his pearly eyes.

'If we destroy the Mole and your people rise up,' Dakkar said, 'we may be able to take Cryptos by surprise. Now bow before me.'

'What?' Olszar said, looking bewildered.

'I said, bow before me, dog!' Dakkar said, raising his voice and pushing Olszar down.

Olszar fell to his knees and grabbed the jacket, pushing it behind the feet of his comrades. 'Forgive me, Prince Dakkar,' Olszar said, not too convincingly.

'Good,' Dakkar said. He turned to the guard. 'Get this dolt back to work. I'll teach him to insult me.'

'Get up!' the guard yelled as Dakkar stalked off.

He glanced back to see his jacket and its contents being carefully slipped behind a large rock. He turned and walked straight into a worker dragging a barrel.

'Pardon me, monsieur,' said the familiar figure, standing straight and then making a slight bow.

'Monsieur Lafitte,' Dakkar said, raising his eyebrows.

The pirate's once-fine clothing hung in rags, and dirt streaked his face. He looked intently at Dakkar.

'You forget that I am a master smuggler,' Lafitte said in French. 'I saw what you did there – the work of an amateur!' He spat on the ground.

'I don't know what you mean,' Dakkar said, his heart thumping. Sweat trickled down his back. 'What do you want?'

'Just for you to know that I am with you and your fishy friends,' Lafitte said, and winked at Dakkar before hefting the barrel on to his shoulder and striding off.

Dakkar's stomach lurched. If Lafitte had noticed, then had any of the guards? He glanced around but they seemed at ease. With Blight out of the way and the impending evacuation of the island, they seemed more relaxed than normal.

There was nothing to be relaxed about though. Dakkar knew that. So much could go wrong in the next few days.

CHAPTER TWENTY-EIGHT
THE WORST LAID SCHEMES

Cryptos kept to his laboratory the next day, leaving Dakkar to wander the jetty unsupervised while Oginski and Fulton worked inside the giant *Nautilus*. Dakkar could hear them through the hatch.

'I'm tellin' you, Frank, I'm worried about Georgia,' Fulton said over the clinking of tools. 'Cryptos hasn't let me talk to her since she went off with Dakkar in the *Liberty*.'

Oginski's head popped up from the hatch and he fixed Dakkar with a steely gaze. 'Why can't we see Georgia? What's going on?' he snapped.

'I don't know. Cryptos hasn't told me. He's working on the Voltalith,' Dakkar said, shrugging and staring at the floor.

He wanted to tell them that she'd escaped, that she was all right – but was she? He hadn't seen her reach the surface. All he knew was that she'd escaped from the *Liberty*. If he told them that now, they might down tools and delay everything. Or do something rash and endanger the slaves in the chamber.

Oginski paused and looked long and hard at Dakkar. 'Why are you doing this?' he asked softly.

'Why did you lie to me?' Dakkar said, his breath quickening and tears stinging his eyes.

'Sometimes we have to lie to those we care about,' Oginski murmured. Shaking his head, he disappeared back into the *Nautilus*.

'Then that's your answer,' Dakkar whispered, and rushed from the jetty before he gave in and told Oginski everything.

Time dragged by. Dakkar wandered the quiet corridors. He even tried to see what Cryptos was doing in his laboratory but his guards blocked the way. He crept up the vent at the side of the chamber and looked down on the toiling slaves. Few of them were actually carrying things now. The last barrels of gunpowder were being rolled up the side tunnels. Gangs of exhausted slaves sat gasping at the side of the chamber, watched over by armed guards. Blight stalked those poor souls still working.

Dakkar squinted, making out the lines of what he thought was fuse wire leading from each side tunnel to a central core near the Mole. Presumably, once the Mole had dug deep enough, the fuse would be lit and the whole island would go up. He crawled back out of the tunnel and returned to his room, thankful that it was late and time to sleep. Tomorrow would be a big day. Only

a handful of guards remained in the volcano now. The
others had been sent elsewhere. Dakkar frowned. *Where
to?* he thought. Cryptos must have another base like this.
His stomach tightened as the thought struck him. His
brothers may be there, planning similar schemes, breed-
ing similar monsters. Stopping Cryptos might be only the
beginning of what was necessary.

Dakkar slept badly that night. Worries – about Georgia,
about the explosives in the chamber, about Cryptos –
tangled in his dreams, waking him with a start.

A knock on the door made him leap from his bed.
His heart pounding, he opened it to find Cryptos standing there, gripping a Sea Arrow in each fist. His guards
pointed rifles over his shoulder at Dakkar.

'Well done, my prince,' he sneered. 'You managed to
fool even me for a while but, as the poet Burns would say,
"The best laid schemes of mice and men oft go awry".
And yours, my friend, was not even the best laid of plans.'

Dakkar was marched down the passage and through
the doors into the chamber. Oginski, Fulton and Georgia
sat, tied together, not far from the scaffold that held the
Mole upright and in place.

'Dakkar, I'm sorry,' Georgia burst out, her face tear-
stained and filthy. 'I got to the volcano's rim but . . .'

'Did you think I wouldn't have that entrance guarded?'
Cryptos said, pushing the Sea Arrows into the hands of
the nearest guard. 'My Qualar brought her to me. All it
took was to point a loaded musket at her precious uncle's

head and she told me everything. Weakling!'

'It doesn't matter,' Dakkar said, smiling at Georgia. He turned to Oginski. 'At least you know that I'm not a monster.'

Oginski gave a sad smile back and nodded.

'Not yet, my prince,' Cryptos said, his voice low and full of emotion. 'But what if I leave you alive while these unfortunates fry in here? Would you seek my blood then? Hatred is such an easy emotion to stir in a young heart.'

'No. I feel sorry for you,' Dakkar said, his voice small.

Cryptos swung the back of his hand across Dakkar's face, stinging his cheek.

'Imbecile,' Cryptos spat, running to the foot of the scaffold. 'You'll feel sorry for yourself when today is through.'

He pulled a lever and a low humming vibrated through the Mole machine, the scaffold and then through Dakkar's feet. The massive pointed drill began to rotate, cracking and splintering the rock, its sharp nose biting into the very stone. Faster and faster it turned. The whine became deafening and stone chips sprayed across the chamber, making everyone screw their eyes shut for a second.

The guard holding the Sea Arrows threw his hands to his face as a chip caught him in the eye.

Dakkar spun round and brought his leg high, kicking the man in the side of the head. The guard flew sideways, dropping the explosives. As Dakkar landed, he snatched them from the air and turned to the Mole, hurling the arrows with all his might.

Time seemed to slow. Cryptos lunged forward, his mouth wide, his long fingers clawing at the flying missiles. The arrows arced high above his grasping hands and landed on the scaffold, blossoming into fiery blooms of destruction.

The chamber erupted into a nightmare of fire and deafening explosion, screeching metal and pounding rock. Dakkar felt himself being lifted into the air and hurled across the chamber. Rock and flame stabbed and seared his skin.

And then all fell silent.

Dakkar grunted and rolled over. His whole body ached. His face felt numb and he could taste blood in his mouth.

Rock dust filled the air along with the sound of men's groans. Dakkar staggered to his feet. The huge Mole lay at an angle, half buried in the ground. Rock and twisted metal clung to its cylindrical body. Oginski, Fulton and Georgia lay semi-conscious, their ropes still binding them.

'What . . . have you . . . done?' Cryptos wheezed, standing up. 'All my work, all my plans . . .'

'Even the best laid plans . . .' Dakkar said, smiling grimly.

The rest of the chamber came to life. The guards, their weapons blown from their grasp, backed away from the slaves. The slaves, realising their strength in numbers, began a mumbling, bloodthirsty moan that grew into a full-blooded howl as they charged at the fleeing guards.

'For Qualarium!' Olszar bellowed, lifting one of Cryptos's men above his head and hurling him across the chamber.

Lafitte stood for a second, shrugged, then yelled, 'Vive la France!' He wrenched a pistol from one guard and fired at another.

Bodies flew and pistols cracked as the guards were quickly overwhelmed.

'Give up, Cryptos,' Dakkar said. 'It's finished.'

'Oh, is it?' Cryptos hissed, grabbing a smouldering beam of wood and tossing it at the central fuse that lay at his feet among the wreckage. Eight spurts of fire came to life, racing across the chamber floor. 'You can't put them all out, and the *Nautilus* awaits me. Farewell, Dakkar. You should die knowing what a disappointment you are to me and your father.' Cryptos turned and raced for the door.

Dakkar stood paralysed for a second, contemplating how to extinguish all eight fuses.

Lafitte ran up to him. 'Quickly, mon ami!' he cried, grabbing a knife from one of the unconscious guards. 'We must free your friends and leave while we can.'

Slaves were streaming out of the chamber now, jostling each other to get through the door. Dakkar hurried over and pulled at the ropes as Lafitte sawed at them with the knife. Soon Oginski, Fulton and Georgia clambered to their feet like sleepwalkers.

'What happened?' Fulton groaned.

'There's no time,' Dakkar snapped, pulling Georgia to her feet. 'We've got to go!'

As if to emphasise Dakkar's statement, one low rumble after another shook the chamber.

'The explosives have gone off in the vents!' Dakkar said. 'The whole place will fill with seawater any second!'

At the same time, the Mole gave a hideous screech and began to shudder in the hole it had created when if fell. Dakkar watched in horror as the metal monster twisted and bucked out of the hole, bouncing across the floor with a deafening clang. The crumpled drill was spinning freely again, sending the machine careering around the chamber like a tornado.

'Let's go!' Lafitte screamed. 'Allez!'

They stumbled towards the door and out into the corridor. Behind them came the scream of tortured metal and the rush of water. A colossal bang blasted down the passage, almost knocking them off their feet. Then the doorway collapsed as the seawater drove the whirling drill through the wall and after them.

CHAPTER TWENTY-NINE
DEATH CHASE

The tunnel behind them was a boiling cauldron of death. Water roared, forcing the screeching steel monster through the tunnels. Rock splinters and sparks spat after them as the Mole scoured at the walls. The whole volcano shook and lumps of rock fell from the ceiling as they hurled themselves down the passage.

'Head for the cavern!' Fulton shouted. 'Even if Cryptos has taken the *Nautilus*, the *Liberty* might still be there.'

The Mole gave a mighty clang and wedged in the tunnel for a second, plugging it completely.

Lafitte stopped and bent over, catching his breath. 'Mon Dieu,' he panted. 'Thank goodness it has stopped.'

'Come on, we must hurry!' Dakkar yelled, running back to grab Lafitte's elbow. 'It's not safe. This whole volcano is going to collapse.'

'Pfft!' Lafitte said, waving him away. 'I cannot run another step –'

A threatening groan of rock cut him short. The Mole's buckling body creaked and slid a little. Water began to hiss round the edge of the crumpled steel, making the contact between metal and rock slippery.

'Quickly!' Dakkar howled, and sprinted after the others.

Lafitte followed as the Mole gave another complaining squeal and continued its pell-mell journey down the tunnel.

The light of the cavern shining at the end of the tunnel seemed miles away to Dakkar. The rumbling behind him filled his senses but yet again the Mole clanged to a sudden halt.

This time Lafitte didn't stop running. Dakkar half ran, half fell through the door of the cavern and crashed into the backs of Oginski and Fulton.

They stood stock-still, staring at Cryptos and two of his guards, who levelled guns at them.

'Ever resourceful,' Cryptos snarled. 'Never dying.'

His brother shrugged. 'Well, I am an Oginski,' he replied. 'You should know how hard we are to kill.'

All the while, Oginski was edging them away from the cavern entrance. Dakkar, Georgia, Fulton and Lafitte kept close behind him, shuffling quietly, trying not to look back up the tunnel. Now they stood clear of the doorway, leaving Cryptos and his guards exposed.

'But your time has run out,' Cryptos bragged. 'You did a good job on the *Nautilus* for me.'

Something grated and crashed up the corridor but the guards were watching Oginski intently.

'With a section of the Voltalith fitted to the engine, it has four times the power,' Oginski agreed, backing away a little. 'But it shouldn't be used for war, Kazmer.'

Another roar echoed down the tunnel.

'And what should it be used for,' Cryptos sneered, 'if not for building a new world? This is just a setback, Oginski, you know that. If it's not me, then one of our brothers will continue the work.'

The thundering grew louder.

'Please, Kazmer,' Oginski said, taking a step forward. 'The volcano is collapsing. The Mole is destroyed. Your plan is foiled. I beg you, my brother, give this up.'

'Don't move,' Cryptos said, waving a finger at Oginski. 'I've had enough of your sanctimonious snivelling. Guards!'

The men levelled their rifles. Dakkar flinched, turning his head away as the men prepared to fire.

The explosion deafened Dakkar. For the second time, he was thrown on to his back as the Mole burst through the doorway in a shower of rock and seawater. His last vision of Cryptos was of his shocked face, the man's slick, bloodied hands grappling at the Mole's buckled tip as it whirled through him. Then guards, Cryptos, rock and Mole machine plunged into the lagoon, soaking Dakkar and sending jellyfish splattering across the walls and jetty. Dust and rock splinters blasted from the tunnel entrance and shards tumbled from the ceiling of the cavern.

For a moment, Dakkar stood still with the others, contemplating the twisted wreckage that sank beneath the water.

Cryptos was dead.

'Quickly – we aren't safe yet!' Oginski snapped, and ran along the jetty to the submarines that bucked and rolled in the water. Dakkar followed.

'The whole volcano cone is imploding,' Fulton said above the growing rumble that filled the cavern. 'We need to get out to sea in the subs.'

Fulton and Georgia clambered into the *Liberty* while Dakkar went with Oginski and Lafitte to the *Nautilus*.

The roar of crumbling rock deafened them now. More chunks of stone fell from the shadows above, making the subs pitch even more wildly in the water.

Oginski threw off the ropes and climbed the ladder up the tower that sat in the middle of the *Nautilus*. He pulled the hatch open and began to climb in. He turned to say something but a fragment of rock clipped his temple. Dakkar saw a spurt of blood and Oginski's eyes roll, then Oginski tumbled inside the *Nautilus*.

'Oginski!' Dakkar screamed, and leapt inside the sub.

Lafitte climbed in after him. Oginski lay, pale and groaning, at the foot of the ladder. Lafitte squatted next to him.

'I think he'll be all right,' the pirate said, wiping blood from Oginski's face, 'but you will have to captain the ship.'

Dakkar glanced around. He hadn't really taken in his surroundings. They stood in what was the control room of the *Nautilus*. A large ship's wheel faced portholes that lined the front of the tower. Dakkar went to stand behind the wheel. He recognised the lever next to him and slammed the *Nautilus* to *Full Ahead*. A strange whine filled the ship as the engines powered up.

Something hit the top of the *Nautilus*, making Lafitte cry out. They stumbled, trying to keep their balance as the sub rocked but, slowly, she began to move forward. Dakkar spun the wheel, leaning into it as she veered to port. Ahead he could see the *Liberty* sinking beneath the waves towards the cavern entrance. Twisting another wheel, Dakkar heard the gushing of water filling the ballast tanks and the *Nautilus* also began to submerge.

Many of the glowing jellyfish had been hit by the falling rocks and their glow had reduced to a residual glimmer. Dakkar squinted through the glass at the distant rugged arch of blackness that marked the way to open sea. Rocks rained down now, thumping the sides and top of the *Nautilus*. Dakkar and Lafitte flinched with every bang. The entrance grew closer as the clatter of stones on the roof increased. A porthole cracked but held against the pressure of the water outside. Lafitte crouched, holding Oginski, who groaned as he came to.

The sea boiled as more of the cavern roof collapsed. A fog of bubbles and muck clouded Dakkar's vision. He caught brief glimpses of Qualar flitting in and out, dodging falling stones and fleeing for the sea too. He also saw the outline of bodies floating lifelessly in the water, blood seeping from their wounds and drawing all manner of scavenger fish despite the turmoil of the cave's collapse. He tried not to look too closely.

The surge of the current through the sea cave rocked the *Nautilus* sideways and Dakkar clung to the wheel. Something smashed down on to the back of the sub, making the engine stutter for a second.

'Mon Dieu!' Lafitte yelled. 'We are going to sink!'

A massive arch from the cavern entrance plunged before them, setting the *Nautilus* on a collision course. Dakkar slammed the sub into reverse, but their forward momentum could only be slowed. The shadow of the rock filled the front portholes. Dakkar squeezed his eyes shut and dragged the wheel back, forcing the sub upward as they slid towards the rock. The *Nautilus* shuddered, scraping her belly across the stony surface as she skimmed the obstacle. Then the bright sunlight from above streamed in through the portholes.

'We're clear, mes amis!' Lafitte laughed, clapping his hands. 'You did it!'

'What happened?' Oginski moaned. 'What hit me?'

Dakkar pushed the *Nautilus* to *Full Ahead* again and nearly fell over as she surged forward. They powered through the water, overtaking the tiny *Liberty*. Dakkar caught a glimpse of Georgia waving through the porthole, and then he was lost in a sea of bubbles and startled shoals of fish.

He guided the sub to the surface and emptied the ballast. The daylight dazzled him. In the distance, he could see the volcano sinking into itself with a distant roar. An explosion of bright orange lava boiled up from the shattered cone, followed by a vast plume of dust coiling up to the sun.

'We did it,' Dakkar gasped and slumped against the wheel.

CHAPTER THIRTY
FOND FAREWELLS

The *Nautilus* rocked as the waves from the exploding island reached them. Gradually the explosion died down, leaving only the smouldering wreckage of the volcano, and Dakkar steered the craft back towards the island. Oginski sat up now, an improvised bandage round his head.

'It should be safe on the beach,' he said, wincing and touching his temple. 'We must salvage any provisions we can before we set off anywhere else.'

'And you must rest, Oginski,' Dakkar said, nervously eyeing the red stain on the bandage.

'We all need to rest,' Oginski said with a tight smile.

A fine mist of dust and steam clouded their view but they headed for the beach, towards a wooden pier that jutted out into the sea.

They docked next to the *Liberty*, where Georgia and Fulton waited, accompanied by a small group of survivors – Qualar and human.

Dakkar grinned as he waved to Georgia through the porthole and almost pushed Oginski over as he hurried to the ladder. They climbed out on to the pier, Dakkar relishing the sun on his face.

'Well, mes amis,' Lafitte declared, stretching his arms and smoothing out his torn clothes. 'That was another successful mission for Captain Lafitte. Now, once we are replenished with the supplies, I will show you the way home.'

'You good-for-nothing pirate!' Georgia yelled, stamping up to Lafitte and clenching her fists at her sides. 'If you hadn't tried to take us prisoner and sell us in the first place, then –'

'Georgia, please!' Fulton said, putting an arm round her shoulders. 'Give the man a chance. He did help us to escape, after all.'

Dakkar grinned up at Oginski, who returned the smile.

'You did well, Dakkar,' Oginski said, then his smile faded. 'I thought I'd lost you back there.'

'It didn't turn out quite how I planned it,' Dakkar muttered, feeling his cheeks reddening.

'I meant before that,' Oginski said, squeezing Dakkar's shoulder. 'I meant when you said you'd be Cryptos's apprentice.'

'I'm sorry for deceiving you,' Dakkar said, looking down at the planks of the pier.

'And I for deceiving you,' Oginski said, lifting Dakkar's chin up. 'Will you return to your father?'

'I don't know,' Dakkar said, tears stinging his eyes. 'It might be safer.'

'You could be right,' Oginski said, glancing around. His eyes lingered on the smouldering mound of the volcano. 'Kazmer was still my brother. I can remember when we were children, when times were good.'

'I'm sorry, Oginski,' Dakkar said. 'You mustn't blame yourself for Cryptos's death.'

'No, it couldn't be avoided,' Oginski said, blinking back the tears. 'But I can't help thinking that my other brothers are out there. Will every encounter with them end in death?'

'Who can tell?' Dakkar murmured, shaking his head.

The sea around the pier bubbled and Georgia gasped. Qualar clambered out of the water. Dakkar recognised Olszar. He had a wreath of red coral round his head.

'Dakkar,' he said, gripping the boy's hand. 'You're safe! We searched for you as best we could but in all the confusion . . .'

'You're free from Cryptos now,' Dakkar said, bowing to Olszar. 'Will your people unite?'

Olszar gave what Dakkar took to be a shrug. 'Who knows?' he said. 'Cryptos has tainted our people with his trickery. Mankind's forays into the sea grow bolder every day, and once the ways of greed and avarice are learned they are hard to put aside.'

'That is too true,' Dakkar said. 'Just remember that we aren't all bad.'

'You have a special place in our hearts, Prince Dakkar,' Olszar said, raising his voice. He pointed to the coral wreath. 'I, as Shoal Lord of Qualarium, recognise Prince Dakkar as a friend of our people. No Qualar shall turn him away or deny him assistance!'

The beach resounded with cheers and Dakkar stood amazed as heads popped up from the water.

'You should stay here for a while,' Olszar said. 'We can get whatever you need.'

'The *Nautilus* is ready to sail,' Oginski said. 'But I'm not sure about the *Liberty*.'

'She's always ready,' Fulton laughed, slapping Oginski's shoulder. 'But we need supplies and rest.'

'Wait a minute,' Georgia butted in. 'How come *they* get to take the big boat away?'

'The *Liberty* is ours,' Fulton said, putting his hands on his hips. 'Oginski and Dakkar haven't got their own craft.'

'I'll send full plans and descriptions of the *Nautilus*, Robert, you can be sure,' Oginski laughed. 'I won't forget. Otherwise I think Georgia would swim across the ocean to remind me!'

The Qualar set up a camp on the beach made from things they rescued from the wreckage. Over the next few days, they dragged items and useful pieces of wood out of the sea and on to the sand.

Other men had escaped from the cavern and were refitting a small ship that was moored at the jetty. Lafitte fell in with them and took the role of captain upon himself before anyone could object.

'We shall head for the Bay of Barataria,' he told the men as they hammered and sawed at the planks, 'land of beautiful women and mountains of treasure!'

Dakkar was also able to get to know the *Nautilus*. The ship handled differently to the little *Makara* and Oginski was loath to let Dakkar sail her.

'Wait until we're properly out to sea,' he said, not meeting Dakkar's eye.

The *Nautilus* looked very much like the *Liberty* inside, only the large space below deck was split into different cabins and storerooms. The captain's cabin at the top was in the form of a tower, with viewing windows across the front.

'The upper cabin doesn't detach from the rest, like in the *Makara*,' Dakkar said, pulling a face. 'I think a smaller craft may be more useful sometimes.'

'A good point,' Oginski said. 'I might look into that when we get home.'

What impressed Dakkar most was the hatch at the bottom of the ship. A hatch opened into a separate small chamber which could be sealed and filled with water once someone was inside.

'It's rather like the lock on a canal system,' Fulton had explained. 'It means that you can swim out of the sub without it having to surface.'

Finally, the *Nautilus* and *Liberty* were stocked with food and water. Georgia and Dakkar walked along the beach towards the pier. They had wandered in silence for some time. Dakkar listened to the hiss and splash of the waves. Somewhere above, a seagull cried as it flew.

'I'm sorry for lying to you,' Dakkar said at last.

'You had to,' Georgia murmured. 'It's the way of the world, it seems.'

'I'd never actually have released those eels, you know,' he said. 'I just had to convince Cryptos I was on his side and I was fairly sure he still needed you alive.'

'Fairly sure?' Georgia said, raising her eyebrows and pouting her lip. 'That's comforting to know!'

'Well, certain then!' Dakkar declared.

'That sounds better.' She smiled.

'But thank you for saving my life,' Dakkar added.

'Um, which time are you thanking me for?' Georgia said, wrinkling her nose.

'All of them,' Dakkar said. 'Maybe I should make a long-winded, pompous speech about how much I owe you and how the people of Bundelkhand will be forever grateful to you for saving Prince Dakkar!'

'It's all right,' Georgia replied. 'I get the idea.'

'Will you keep in touch?' Dakkar asked. 'And let me know what you're doing?'

'Sure,' Georgia said. 'And I bet it won't be long before we meet up again.'

'I don't know,' Dakkar said, kicking a pebble into the waves. 'I'm not sure if I should go back to my father.'

'Your father wants you to learn how to be a good leader, right?' Georgia said, stopping on the sand and touching Dakkar's arm.

'Yes,' Dakkar nodded, frowning.

'And is Oginski teaching you that?' she asked.

'Yes, but . . .'

'Well, you know what to do,' Georgia cut in, and carried on walking.

'I'll miss you, Georgia Fulton,' Dakkar said, bowing.

Georgia laughed and curtseyed. 'Why, thank you, your highness!'

Olszar stood on the jetty, waiting for them to board. Fulton and Oginski gripped each other's hands.

'I'll race you to Florida,' Fulton said, and clambered into the *Liberty*.

'I think we might win!' Oginski called after him, and climbed into the *Nautilus*.

Dakkar gave a final wave to Georgia and followed Oginski. The *Nautilus* hummed with power as they submerged.

'So, what's it to be?' Oginski murmured once the open sea rocked the sub. 'India or England?'

'You've taught me a lot, Oginski,' Dakkar said, staring out of the porthole at the quivering pattern of sunlight through the waves.

'This has probably been your most interesting lesson so far,' Oginski said, smiling briefly. 'But there's a lot more to learn.'

'Then set a course for England, Count Oginski.' Dakkar grinned. 'And here's to an adventurous education!'

A NOTE FROM THE AUTHOR

CAPTAIN NEMO

Prince Dakkar grew up to become Captain Nemo, the tormented anti-hero. I first met Captain Nemo when I was about eight or nine years old and, I have to confess, it wasn't in the book but in the 1950s Disney film *20,000 Leagues Under the Sea*. I was mesmerised by the adventure, the giant squid attacks, the underwater cities, the *Nautilus* and everything about it! Another film that popped up on Saturday afternoon television was *The Mysterious Island*, which also featured Captain Nemo. (That one had a giant crab in it.)

A copy of *Twenty Thousand Leagues Under the Sea* by Jules Verne lurked around the house, and here's another confession: I really struggled reading it at that age. But Captain Nemo captured my imagination and has haunted me ever since.

He's a man who has turned his back on the world, vowing never to set foot on dry land ever again. He's a genius, an engineer, an artist, an athlete, sometimes a pacifist, sometimes a righter of wrongs. He hates colonialism and he invents the *Nautilus*. I always wondered how Nemo learned all these things, and how he came to be so disenchanted with the world.

Some critics say the strength of Jules Verne's work lies in his inventiveness and his inclusion of what was, at the time, cutting-edge science. His were some of the earliest works of what we now call science fiction. Detractors often dismiss his stories from the point of view of plot or character. It is true that some of Verne's characters are stereotypes and one-dimensional, but nobody could say that about Captain Nemo!

THE CALL OF THE SEA!
(OR NOT)

I grew up on a peninsula and so the sea was never very far away. Add this to the fact that my father and brothers were always messing about in boats and it's small wonder I was fascinated by the sea. Or at least the *idea* of the sea. I was a terrible swimmer and didn't like getting cold and wet (what a wimp!). But I loved reading about monsters of the deep and submarines either in books or comics. My first ambition was to be an underwater archaeologist. I didn't know then if such people actually existed but I wanted to be one.

RESEARCH

And so, forty years later, I found myself trying to think what I would like to write next for Bloomsbury. Something historical and under the sea . . . underwater archaeology . . . Captain Nemo resurfaced and the research that I did threw up some interesting surprises!

The first thing I had to do was work out when Nemo was born and what would have been happening in the world when he was growing up. This proved a little more complicated than I first imagined.

Jules Verne's *Twenty Thousand Leagues Under the Sea* and *The Mysterious Island* follow each other in terms of events. In the first, we meet Nemo and his amazing submarine, the *Nautilus*. But somehow the dates in the two books had become confused. So, in *Twenty Thousand Leagues Under the Sea*, a hale and hearty Nemo is charging around the undersea world between 1866 and 1868. In *The Mysterious Island* Verne says that after the events of *Twenty Thousand Leagues Under the Sea*, Nemo docks the *Nautilus* under a volcanic island for six years, awaiting his death, and that he died on 15th October 1868. Obviously the dates don't add up here! Scholars have blamed Verne's editors for the confusion as the great man himself was a stickler for detail.

However, Verne does say that Nemo was sixty when he decided to stop sailing and await death. He waited six years, so he would have been sixty-six when he died in 1868. The year of his birth was therefore 1802. I've taken the liberty of being a little flexible with Nemo's age. He is around thirteen – or maybe an 'old' twelve – in 1814 in my story. I hope readers will forgive this flagrant disregard for the dates!

Two of the characters, Robert Fulton and Jean Lafitte, aren't fictional. Robert Fulton was an American inventor and is credited with creating the first working submarine in 1800, which he called . . . the *Nautilus*! He also invented the floating steam battery.

Jean Lafitte was a French privateer who operated out of Grand Terre Island off the coast of Louisiana. He became something of a hero when he helped the Americans defeat the British at the Battle of New Orleans.